WHAT DREAMS MAY COME

JAMESON HOLLYBROOK

AUTHOR'S NOTE

What Dreams May Come is an erotic Dark Fantasy novella that contains death and explicit scenes of sexual acts and torture, including a brief scene of a sexual interaction during torture.

ONE

I BALANCE THE TRAY of food carefully and tilt my head to the side, letting my hair obscure my face as I walk around the back of the club. It's as boisterous as ever, music loud and silk clothes being tossed from the stage, though there aren't many patrons on the main floor tonight. Very few of them are next to the bar, making my attempt to sneak onto one of the balconies successful. All the booths *here* are full—but none of them are the man I need to hide from, and the man I want to hide *with* sits at the booth in the back corner. It's a good spot for him, books open as he works here instead of his office; it's a good spot for me, the view from this balcony notoriously terrible and giving patrons plenty of privacy. No one will see me with Armel. *Mikael* won't see me.

Armel sits with his head propped against one hand, scribbling in one book as he references the others. His long, russet-colored hair is tucked behind pointed ears and draped over one shoulder, the ends of it threatening to brush against the wet ink on his page, but he looks up before it can. "Are you serving our guests tonight?" he asks as I approach, with a smile that reveals sharp eyeteeth.

I push a book aside to set down my tray. "Only you. I was told you've been sitting here for six hours without moving."

"And serving me helps you avoid the Trahan boys down below."

I wince, shoving the tray towards him before stealing a piece of roasted asparagus from it and pouring him more wine. "I was hoping you hadn't seen them," I say softly, sitting next to him.

He drinks his wine slowly, staring at me. "Do you have their money?"

"I will by the end of tonight."

"And how do you plan on making that money?" he asks, head tilting to the side. "You aren't scheduled for the stage." I gesture to my body lazily. "Without Mikael noticing you?"

I nod and push the tray towards him again. "Eat. I don't want to get yelled at."

"Marsaili won't yell at you," he replies, but he obediently eats a piece of steak. "She thinks you're the only one I won't bite when she sends someone to feed me."

I snort, glancing at an open book—names and numbers, quick notes and collected information—but Armel closes it before I can see too many details. I stare at his long fingers on the cover before I slowly lift my gaze. "You don't bite," I say. "She knows better."

His lips quirk up in a small smile. "How are you planning on making the money you owe?"

"Offering myself to someone who's not Mikael," I answer. "And yes, without him noticing me."

He nods and looks me over, raising one brow. I scoff lightly, bending over to unbuckle my boots and remove them. Armel sits back as I lean against the booth to lift my hips and wiggle out of tight trousers. After a moment of watching me struggle, he snorts and pushes on my chest until I'm laying across the seat, my legs across his lap. He tugs on the hems of my trouser legs gently, a faint smile on his lips again. I shove my trousers down, letting him pull them off. His fingertips ghost across my skin, and I shiver. He places a hand under my knees as he pulls my legs free, then neatly folds my trousers and sets them aside. I stare up at the ceiling for a moment before slowly sitting up. His fingers barely touch me and I'm ready to pray to the gods for succor.

"I'll put your things in my office," he says. "Your coat?"

I finger the collar as I consider it, then remove it and pass it to him before getting on my knees and holding my arms out for inspection. "Well?"

He looks me over.

First he takes my bracelets and my rings, summoning a box from the air around us to hold them. My fluorite earrings stay, as does the matching necklace. A thin chain necklace is removed, though, and placed amongst the other jewelry. "Are you sure about this?" he asks as he opens the neckline of my shirt. His fingers move along my chest slowly, lingering along the edges of light, twin scars under my breasts. I almost shiver again.

"No," I admit. "But I don't have many other choices."

His lashes lower. "You could allow me to buy your debt from Mikael."

I hesitate, then shake my head. "I don't want to be indebted to a fay lord."

"You know my bargains aren't as terrible as others."

"I do, and my answer is still no."

He sighs. "The offer remains on the table."

"I know," I reply as I slide out of the booth. It's been there since he first heard of my debt.

"Jocelyn," he says. It's the tone that makes me stop—soft and curiously mild, enough to make me turn around. Armel crooks one finger to beckon me closer, and I crawl along the booth to straddle his lap.

He places one finger under my chin, turning my face this way and that before brushing a soft, quick kiss to my lips. Warmth curls throughout me. "Be careful whose attention you draw, ash tree boy."

"Any suggestions?" I ask, though I'm tempted to stay put. The thought of curling under his arm to bask in his attention is an alluring one, but the thought of being indebted to him keeps me from melting under his touch.

"The Chastain bookkeeper is here." His finger moves from my chin, trailing down my neck to my chest. "On the other balcony, far from the Trahan boys. He's watched you before, pet."

I stare past Armel as I try to remember the bookkeeper's face. "Do you actually think he's a wise choice, or do you just want information?"

Armel smiles.

It's answer enough.

I roll my eyes, pulling away from him—but I don't get the chance to go far before he grabs my leg. I hold still as my leg is lifted, shirt pushed up so Armel can place a kiss high on my inner thigh. Then he *bites*.

I gasp, gripping his shoulders tightly as I try not to squirm. He sucks, soothes the spot with his tongue. I cling to the back of the booth as he sits up and smirks, running a thumb along his lip to wipe away a spot of blood. *Damn* him. I don't know how to move, unable to stop staring at him as he licks the blood away and warmth spreads throughout me. I don't know if I should be indignant or not. I *really* want him to do it again. Maybe I should stay put and let him buy my debt from Mikael—no. *No.*

Absolutely horrible idea. Especially with how smug Armel looks, watching me as I slide out of the booth. I shake my head at him, trying to look as disapproving as Marsaili would. Armel's smile only grows. The fay are possessive, *particularly* when they have Armel's heritage.

I send a thanks to every god whose name I can remember that my knees don't give out as I walk away from him.

My shirt hides Armel's bite easily, though I take a moment downstairs to examine just how noticeable the bruise is—and it is *glaringly* so against my fair skin. I sigh and step into the club again, watching Mikael's table warily as I make my way to the other balcony. I stop and hide when his men walk around the room, smiling when I finally reach the stairs and can dash up them to hide behind a pillar on the balcony. I peek around it, down at Mikael and his men in their booth. The man is as relaxed as only a merchant prince of the City can be, looking bored by the show on the stage. Smoking and drinking away his wealth, might fuck it away if I'm busy for hours.

I turn away with a frown to look at the booths along this balcony. As they were on the other, they're all full, but there's no question which one holds the Chastain men. Three personal guards linger along the balcony, surreptitiously watching the stage. One booth holds five men while the others hold only couples lost in each other. I watch the booth, the guards, for a moment, then push away from the pillar to approach slowly. One guard looks at me, eyes narrowing. I smile at him and spin slowly, lifting my shirt slightly. He scoffs, waving a hand at me, and goes back to watching the stage.

The men within the booth are immediately silent when I stand before them.

Two stare, barely able to look away from my legs. A third ignores me—one of the Chastain men, though his name is beyond me. I ignore him in return, and the first two men, turning my attention to the others. Yves Chastain, eldest son of the family and perhaps the smartest merchant they've had in decades; handsome, brown hair to his shoulders and brown eyes that watch me curiously. His nose was broken in his youth during a hunt, and though it healed better than his leg did, it's still slightly crooked. Next to him is Nikolay Voronin, the frighteningly loyal bookkeeper who simply appeared in the City one night. Yves runs a hand through his hair as he considers me, while Nikolay lights a cigarette, staring at me with cold, dark eyes. He blows smoke into the air slowly.

Armel could have sent me to any of them, but he picked Nikolay. I smile at Yves and step up onto the booth's seat, then over him to reach Nikolay. The man stares at me as I settle in his lap, throwing my arm over his shoulder. When I run my finger along the side of his face, tracing the line of a high, sharp cheekbone, he only takes a slow drag on his cigarette and looks at Yves.

"You were saying?" Nikolay asks. I smile and rest my head against his shoulder.

"I was saying you have three weeks," Yves says to the men who have yet to stop staring at me.

One of them snaps to attention. "We need longer than that."

"Why?"

The men glance at each other before the one speaks again. "There has been illness amongst the families, sir, and blight amongst the crops. We don't have the money."

"And we're not asking for it right now," Nikolay drawls. "Three weeks without an increase in interest. Is that not fair?"

The man gapes at Nikolay like a fish, then glances at me. "No increase is very—we aren't sure how the illness—*apologies*, should we be talking about this with *him* here?"

Yves glances at me, then dryly says, "The only person he's going to tell anything to is Armel and Armel already knows why we're meeting. But since you're bothered by him, we'll continue this discussion tomorrow in my office."

"You can bring what money you do have then," Nikolay adds. He takes another drag on his cigarette, glancing at me. I bat my lashes at him.

Yves nods. "You may go."

The men trip over themselves to thank Yves as they stand and leave. Yves watches them go, then snatches the cigarette from Nikolay and takes a deep drag on it. The man who'd ignored me sits back with a groan, hand covering his eyes. Nikolay rests his arms along the back of the booth. I toy with the neckline of his shirt, the collar of his coat, and smile when he looks at me under lowered lashes. He looks bored, the harsh lines of his face giving him a cold beauty. I slide my hand along his neck, closing the distance between us.

"*Why* did Armel send you?"

I kiss Nikolay's cheek, glancing at Yves. "He didn't send me."

"No?" Yves asks. He doesn't wait for a response, cigarette between his lips as he opens my shirt to examine my chest. He lifts the hem of my shirt next and reveals the bruise, raising a brow at me and running his finger over it.

"I'm simply here to entertain," I say, hand moving to the back of Nikolay's neck, then to his short, dark hair.

Yves smiles as he slides from the booth. One of his guards grabs his cane and offers it to him once he's standing, stepping away when Yves takes it. "Entertain Nikolay, then," he says, beckoning for the other man to join him. "He so rarely leaves his office."

Nikolay scoffs quietly, but doesn't argue as he's left alone with me. "Well, you heard my order," I say, running my fingers along his jaw. He looks more like he belongs to the realms of the dead than the realms of the living with how slim and pale he is.

And he looks at me with the same interest the dead have.

"I don't need entertainment," he says.

"What do you need?"

"I have business to attend to."

I shrug, sitting up and straddling his lap. "That doesn't answer my question."

He almost smiles. "What information do you have?"

I smile. "Who are you meeting with next?"

"Hubert Desjardins."

"Did you know," I start, leaning closer to trace my fingers over his lips, "he keeps a secret lover?"

"You'll have to think of something else."

I put my mouth against his ear. "His lover is the son of his wife's closest confidante. He also doesn't know his wife is pregnant but trying to get rid of the babe."

"The father?"

"Hubert's lover."

He looks me over slowly. I sit up, leaning back against the table to let him look his fill. His hands drop to my legs and I shift my hips in anticipation, but all he does is push my shirt up to reveal the bruise again. I keep my gaze up, hoping Armel can hear the curses I think in his direction. Awful, possessive man—and oh, Nikolay is tracing the shape of the bite mark. I look down, watching his long, thin finger. I try not to shiver. His touch is a featherlight tease that's gone too soon as he drapes his arms over the back of the booth again.

"If that's true, I'll pay you to sit here and tell me what you know about everyone else I'm meeting with," he says.

I smile again. "I cost a thousand golden stars."

Nikolay smiles back, coldly amused. "No, you don't."

"I do tonight."

He has the audacity to scoff. "A thousand silver crescents."

I laugh. "I make more than that on stage!" His smile is a little less cold. I grin as I drape my arms over his shoulders. "Five hundred golden stars, then.

You'll be meeting people *all night*. Pay me for my time."

"We'll see if you're worth that much. What's the lover's name?"

"Antoine."

"Behave. Hubert's coming."

I roll my eyes, but I sit across his lap with my head on his shoulder again and watch as Hubert approaches the booth. The man pauses, glancing at me, then steels himself and slides into the booth.

"I spoke with Yves as I came up here," Hubert says, meeting Nikolay's gaze evenly. He twists a ring nervously as Nikolay remains silent. "He said he would think about giving me leniency on the loan."

"And even if he does, you'll pay as you're meant to," Nikolay says. "Or Antoine's messes with you and your wife will become public knowledge."

Hubert pales, though he tries to look unbothered. "My wife?"

"I hear congratulations are in order. Are you looking forward to being a father?"

Hubert looks bloodless. He gets up stiffly, mumbling about having money the next time he meets with someone. I run my hand through Nikolay's hair, brushing my lips against his jaw.

"Two hundred golden stars for now," Nikolay says. "I'll consider the other three in a few hours."

I kiss him to seal the bargain. "Deal."

He bites my lip, then holds my jaw to keep me still as he leans away. "*Behave.*"

I smile and nod instead of biting his hand.

The Chastain family does business with all sorts of people, and Nikolay meets with anyone from small human families to elves and creatures I can't name. I stay silent through most of them, but there are a few whose secrets I whisper to Nikolay. A woman whose concoctions use fay blood; she turns red and glances at me when Nikolay asks about that. I twirl a lock of Nikolay's hair around my finger as I look back at her. A man whose assistant he hired last year is the daughter his wife's been hiding for years; he looks shocked, turns wary when Nikolay makes an offer on behalf of the Chastain family to educate the girl. It's too good an offer for him to decline, though, and he makes a request to bargain with Yves directly before he goes. An elven man attempts to charm Nikolay with gifts that get passed directly to me—a pearl necklace, an ivory comb, a charmed arrow quiver.

Nikolay smokes and drinks throughout his meetings, even ordering food for the table during one meeting that takes so long I end up dozing with my head on his shoulder. Armel can get his information from someone else. Nikolay jostles me awake after that meeting, blowing cigarette smoke away from me. "A thousand golden stars," he says.

I raise my brows. "What changed your mind?"

"You're valuable just for how much they want to get away when they see you."

I stare at him, unsure of how to take that, then shrug and nod as I reach for wine. "A thousand golden stars."

"Do you want to pay Mikael Trahan now or later?" he asks, watching me from the corner of his eye. He says it so softly.

I nearly knock the wine over. "What?"

Fool, some part of me says as I look over at the man next to me. He watches me like he's watched everyone who sits with him, a predator assessing its prey. Armel gets the same look sometimes, but I know Armel. I don't know Nikolay. No one outside the Chastain family knows much about him, and even then it seems only Yves knows anything. He's not human, though—not human, not fay, not elven, not any creature Armel knows about.

Nikolay Voronin arrived in the City one night and had his name being whispered with fear and awe by the next.

He puts his cigarette out and drinks the whiskey in his glass. "That's who you're indebted to, isn't it?"

I drink a little wine to give myself time to form an answer. "It is . . ."

"Pay him now, or pay him later? I'm keeping you until dawn."

It takes me a moment to catch up. "Later, but I didn't agree to stay with you until *dawn*."

He tucks my hair behind an ear before guiding my mouth to his. "What I want to do to you will take that long."

I follow after him for another kiss as I straddle his lap again. "How many more meetings do you have?"

His hands fall to my legs. "I'm not needed anymore tonight," he says, and the fingers of one hand start to move up along my thigh slowly. I grip the booth behind him, inhaling sharply when his hand slips under my shirt and pushes down against the bruise. His fingers dance along the line of my underclothes next.

I open my legs a little more.

He smirks.

I stare back, refusing to buckle under that smirk or his touch—but my breath hitches as two of his fingers slip beneath my underclothes, sliding over my cunt. His smirk grows at how easily he can slip one finger into me. I have the sudden urge to claw it off his face, but I hold onto the booth instead, digging my nails into velvet and wood. I hadn't realized how *wet* I'd be, and now I don't want to reveal how else this slight touch might affect me. Especially since Nikolay, absolute bastard, sits with one arm along the back of the booth still and pumps that one finger in and out of me slowly. He looks as unruffled as he was when I first came to the booth.

A throat clears behind me.

Nikolay slides a second finger into me.

The back of my neck begins to burn. I grip the booth a little tighter. Nikolay only tilts his head to the side, looking past me. "What?" he asks.

"Master Yves wishes to speak with you again," a man says softly.

"I'll find him in a bit," Nikolay replies, looking at me again. I meet his gaze steadily, trying not to move as his fingers slowly thrust and curl. My thighs ache from holding still for so long. Nikolay's thumb pushes my underclothes aside to brush over my clit. I want to bite him. Leave a mark on him like Armel left on me.

Abruptly, his smirk disappears, replaced by irritation as he looks past me again. "You're still here."

The underling coughs nervously. "I was told to escort you to him. He—*ah*—he didn't think you'd come on your own."

Nikolay rubs my clit, thrusting his fingers deep. I shudder and bite his shoulder to keep my moan in. "Is that so," he says, voice dangerously soft. That soft voice sends another flood of warmth through me and I drop my head against his shoulder. He sounds like Armel, speaking like that. "Go stand by the stairs," he orders. This corner of the club is quiet enough I can hear the hurried footsteps as the underling retreats. "You bit me," Nikolay murmurs in my ear a moment later.

"You had two fingers buried in me in front of a minion. You can handle one bite," I retort, but I'm unable to hold still now as his fingers move again. I drop my hips, rocking on his fingers and biting my lip to keep from groaning.

He uses his free hand to lift my head, hand under my jaw and thumb pulling my lip free of my teeth. We stare at each other as he grows a little more vigorous in fucking me with his fingers. My eyes flutter shut, opening again when he slides his thumb into my mouth. "Armel must be rolling in money because of you," he says. I bite down. He smiles. "Or not, if you bite everyone."

I take a moment to suck on his thumb before slowly pulling it from my mouth. "*He* bites everyone, not me."

"Ah, so I just bring it out in you?"

"Maybe."

Nikolay thrusts his fingers deeper, thumb rubbing my clit hard. I gasp, rolling my hips down against his hand. "Where will I find you when I'm done with Yves?"

"With Armel," I answer, biting my lip again as I hold onto his arms. "After I've paid Mikael."

"How much do you need for that?"

I shudder as I move against him, his thumb in the perfect spot. "A hundred fifty golden stars."

He nods, then deposits me on the booth next to him. I don't have time to sit up with the way he follows to lean over me. He bites down hard on my neck as his fingers thrust in and out of me rapidly, and I gasp again, clutching his shoulders. His thumb moves against my clit again and I squirm, feeling how close release is. With his hips pushing against me as he holds my legs open, I can imagine all too easily how a night with him will be. How it'd be to have him fuck me into the booth. I want it so bad I can't help the whine that escapes when his fingers leave me, so close to a climax and left without it. He grins at me as he licks his fingers clean, then adjusts my underclothes to cover me properly. I can only stare as he sets a small pouch on the table.

"I'll find you soon," he says as he leaves me alone in the booth.

I don't move, legs spread open as I stare at the ceiling and try to breathe again.

It isn't long before Armel's face floats into my field of vision, and I glare at his grin. He must have moved over to this balcony at some point. "Did you have a good time?" he asks sweetly. "You look like a mess."

"Would you fuck me right now if I asked you to?" I ask. "He's a tease."

"You poor thing." There's no sympathy in his voice. "Do you have Mikael's money?" I nod. "Good," he says, all cheer disappearing as he frowns at the club. "Go find him. He's starting to irritate me. Your brother's here, too."

I almost kick him in my scramble to sit up. "*What?* Dorian hasn't seen me, has he?"

He rolls his eyes. "He was distracted as soon as he walked through the doors."

I stand, snatching up the pouch Nikolay left. Armel whistles, throwing my trousers as I turn to him. My boots sit next to the booth. I mutter a hurried thanks, yanking the trousers on. He idly fusses with my hair as I shove my boots on, nodding when I stand for a quick inspection.

Dorian can wait. I need to find Mikael first.

My stomach flutters when I don't see him at his table, but then I see him stepping out of the club with one of his men. Dorian sits at the bar, smiling at a dancer. He starts to stand when he sees me, but I wave a hand at him to stay seated as I follow Mikael outside. He and his man stand away from the club's entrance under a torch by the mouth of an alley, Mikael leaning against the wall with a hand in his pocket. Both stare at me as I approach, cigarette smoke curling into the air around them.

"My payment," I say, throwing the pouch at Mikael's man.

Mikael waits until the man's finished counting to look at me. "I thought you might avoid me all night," he says, pushing away from the wall. His man pulls a flask out of a pocket, placing the pouch of coins there instead.

"I needed a little extra time."

"Who did you charm?"

"Someone who bought me for the rest of the night," I say, laughing as I turn around. "He's waiting for me now."

I should know better.

Mikael yanks me back, throwing a damp cloth over my mouth and nose as he drags me into the alley. "Let him wait. You and I still have business," he whispers. His man stands under the torch still, smoking as he watches the street for any who might approach as I struggle against Mikael. I don't have anything I could use for a weapon though, Mikael hugging my arms against my body. All I can smell is the sickly sweet cloth, darkness closing in as he holds it tighter against my face.

Fuck, I should really know better.

TWO

I WAKE AGGRAVATINGLY SLOWLY, head pounding. I stare down at my lap, then grimace as I lift my head and my neck cracks. No gag and no blindfold, at least. Ankles and wrists bound to the chair I sit in, the rope tied tight enough to hurt. My back aches from the way I've been sitting while unconscious. My tongue feels heavy, mouth too dry. I shake my head to get my hair from my face, then look around.

Dorian sits across from me, similarly bound. His head is still forward, blond hair hiding his face, but his chest rises and falls evenly, steadily. Fear spikes hard enough to make me dizzy with it, and I have to watch him just *breathe* before I can think and look around again. His knuckles are bruised on one hand. Pride swells that he fought back better than me, but the pride dies quickly since we're both tied to chairs in an incredibly empty, dingy room.

He wakes with a jerk, then groans as he lifts his head. "I thought older brothers were supposed to protect the younger children," he says when he opens his eyes and sees me. He spent time amongst the fay before coming to the club, his eyes lined with kohl and the colorful powder they like to use, some of it glittering under the torchlight.

I swallow spit, run my tongue along my teeth. They used something fay on us—there's a lingering taste of too ripe fruit in my mouth. I hate fay intoxicants. "Can't do much when I've been *drugged*."

He tests the rope around his wrists, then his ankles. "Or when you follow someone like Mikael Trahan outside where Armel can't protect you."

I wrinkle my nose up. "Yell at me later."

"I won't have to. Armel will." He rubs his cheek against his shoulder in an attempt to free the hair stuck to a gloss coating his lips. It doesn't work very well and he ends up pouting at me. "Can you contact him?"

I hold my hands up as best I can. "And how am I supposed to do that?"

He grimaces. I shake my head and look around the room again—wood and stone, the space reminding me of a small hut that one fay lord kept on his lands to house humans that entertained him. Maiwenn used to threaten to give me to him, thinking it'd be the perfect punishment. The fay lord at least decorated the hut. There's nothing on the walls here, no windows to tell us where we are or what time of day it is. Nothing in the corners that we could free ourselves with, and the wood of our chairs is too thick to break apart. There's only one door, and it opens as I examine the room.

Dorian goes completely still, staring at me. I stare at the men who enter—Mikael and the man who'd been with him when they took me. Another two carry a small table in, setting it against a wall before they leave. Mikael shuts and locks the door behind them, staring at me as the other man carries a small pouch to the table, metal and glass knocking against each other. Dorian pales, watching him organize his tools. I grip my chair tight, staring back at Mikael.

No fear. Not in front of the fay and not in front of *him.*

"I paid you," I say.

"You were late," he replies.

I scoff. "I gave you more than enough."

"Cyril."

The other man lifts his head. Mikael makes a small gesture. Cyril abandons his tools to walk over to Dorian, quickly grabbing his finger and pulling it back until a crack sounds. Dorian thrashes and curses. I stare in horror as tears track down his face and he tries to breathe through the pain. Mikael never looks away from me.

"Let him go," I whisper. Mikael raises his brows. "Let him go," I repeat, louder. "You have no issue with Dorian. Only me."

"Lessons are learned so much easier this way," Mikael says as he crosses the room to me. He nods to Cyril. Another of Dorian's fingers is broken, the snap making me flinch. Mikael caresses the side of my face and I flinch again, trying to lean away. "The fay-touched Bellerose boys. My father was *so* happy when you came to me for money."

I glance at Dorian. He breathes heavily, glaring at Mikael, at Cyril, at me. "Lesson learned," I say flatly to Mikael. "You can do whatever you want to me, but let him go."

Mikael smiles as he leans down, smelling of cigarette smoke and cheap alcohol. "I can already do whatever I want to you."

He breaks my fingers himself.

Pain stretches time out. Magic makes it worse.

Cyril is a skilled magic user. He has to be academically trained with the way he can focus his magic as he works. He examines Dorian's unbroken fingers, then breaks another with a sickening crack. Dorian only frowns, staring at Cyril in confusion as Cyril walks away—then Dorian rocks with the pain, breathless as he clenches his jaw. I don't understand completely until Cyril places one hand against my shoulder, the other gripping just above my elbow. He meets my gaze steadily as he takes his hand from my shoulder, then slams his hand against it. The *pop* comes with a familiar pain, but far worse than the time I fell out of a tree as a child. I can't see anything for a moment, vision blurry when I can see again. Cyril doesn't give me any time, another pop sounding and pain flaring again as he heals my shoulder. I bite my lip hard enough I taste blood. He heals my fingers while my body is still ringing with that pain.

I don't know when Mikael leaves us—he's there one moment and gone the next, the pain lancing through my body from Cyril's touch at the back of my neck making it hard to focus as lightning courses through my veins. I forget everything I was taught by the fay and *beg*, promising Cyril anything to make it *stop*. He only gives me an impassive look before taking a blade to Dorian's arm. The room starts to smell of the blood that slowly pools under Dorian, then under me when Cyril brings his dagger to me.

Have you ever wanted to see the inside of your arm, how muscle and bone and fat and tendons connect and make it all work?

Pain makes it hard to appreciate the intricacies of the human body.

I lose all sense of time. Cyril heals Dorian and I both before he finally leaves us. I still shiver from the pain I should be feeling. Dorian's cosmetics are a mess from his tears, streaks of black and blue and green down his face. He closes his eyes, dropping his head back. His breathing slowly goes from ragged to even, but he's too tense to be asleep. I watch the door, gripping the armrests of my chair tightly as I will my body to stop trembling.

"Who do you think is going to yell at you first?"

I glance at Dorian. "What?"

"Who do you think will yell at you first? Malo? Elouan? Maiwenn?"

I snort and stare at the blood under us. "None of them," I answer. "I haven't spoken to any of them in years, remember?"

"They miss you," he says.

The laugh that bubbles up is a bitter one. "Who?" I ask. "Elouan? He's too obsessed with his new ward to remember us. Maiwenn? She's the one who kicked me out and told me to survive on my own. Malo?" I look up, find Dorian frowning at me. "Things were already ending with him when I left because he wanted another wife, and then he sided with Maiwenn."

Dorian looks away, lips pressed together as he blinks away tears. "I know."

"I wish you'd stop playing messenger for them." He shrugs. I sigh, dropping my head back to stare at the ceiling. "Armel will yell at me if we get out of here."

"He likes you too much to yell at you."

I smile a little. "That's why he'll yell at me. Because he likes me."

"Does he like *them?*" he asks. "Maiwenn and the others."

"He likes Elouan. I think. They might be related. He thought Maiwenn was a fool for kicking me out."

"She thought *you* were the fool for accepting his help," he replies. "Wouldn't shut up about him being in exile for a reason. Even Malo got tired of her and fucked off into the woods."

I sit up, tugging on the restraints around my wrists. "Did she say *why* Armel was exiled?" He shakes his head. "Damn," I murmur, both for how tight the rope remains and that Dorian doesn't have the answer.

"He's never told you?"

I give him a grim smile. "If Armel ever dies, that's a secret he'll be taking to his grave."

Dorian smiles a little.

The door opens again. Dorian goes still as stone, as if that'll keep him from being noticed. I stare at this new man. He's not one of Mikael's men, not a member of the Trahan family. He's as rich as them, though. He wears a purple cloak lined with gold over one shoulder, held in place by a pin whose design I can't see clearly—some sort of bird, maybe. His shirt is crisp and white, trousers with as few lines as his shirt. Polished boots with heels that click against the stone floor as he walks into the room and slowly removes his gloves. All the jewelry on him glitters under the torches, necklaces and earrings.

"I didn't believe you," he says, looking at the pool of blood disdainfully. He turns that expression on Mikael, who leans against the doorway and smokes. "You could have cleaned them up."

"Thought you might want to take Joss immediately with how much you paid."

The new man *hmph*s, turning back to me and Dorian. Despite the comment and the look, he doesn't hesitate to step into the blood. The closer he gets, the more I can see his fay heritage—the pointed ears, the too bright eyes, the bone structure that looks like it's been carved from stone. He smiles at me.

"When I heard you ran, I was hoping you'd come to me," he says. "Maiwenn thought you would, then she thought I'd find you and take you in." His lip curls. "Shame you found Armel before me."

"Who are you?" Dorian blurts out, fear momentarily forgotten. "Maiwenn's never spoken about some pompous—"

I jerk against my restraints as the man backhands Dorian, wanting to hit him back. Dorian's still for a moment, then his tongue moves along the inside of his cheek and he leans over to spit blood onto the man's boots. I look to the ceiling helplessly. My dear sweet brother. Absolute idiot. He used to get in fights with Malo like this—but he was never tied to a chair when he baited Malo. When Dorian looks up and meets the man's gaze evenly, there's no trace of the fear that Mikael and Cyril had inspired.

The fear curls down my spine instead as the man slowly grins, revealing fangs.

"Tell your man to bring a chair, Mikael," he says. "I changed my mind about taking Joss. I might take this one instead."

Dorian and I stare at each other.

Cyril returns with two chairs, one for Mikael and one for the vampire. Mikael tosses his cigarette aside and shuts the door, locking us all in. The vampire caresses the side of Dorian's face. Dorian leans away, glaring at the floor as the vampire walks to his chair.

"Let Dorian go," I say to Mikael, though I have no hope he'll listen to me now.

Mikael gestures for Cyril to begin again.

Dorian and I turn stubborn this time, clenching our jaws and holding back our cries of pain as Cyril works. Dorian still shudders with the pain; I cry from it, taste blood from biting my lip too hard again. There are splinters under my nails, the skin around my wrists chafed by the rope and blood. I pray to gods whose names I barely know. I learn what I prefer when Cyril works on me—the breaking of a finger over a knife so sharp I don't feel it. A stab over a slow, deliberate cut that runs down the length of my arm, my face, from my hip to my knee. Anything over a nail being ripped away.

Cyril makes a mistake once, getting close enough I can headbutt him. He rears back, staring at me incredulously as he holds his hand over his now broken nose. Dorian laughs. So does the vampire. Mikael looks *furious*. I smile at Cyril.

He hits me hard enough I see stars. It's easier to keep my head down after.

"Perhaps that's enough of that," the vampire says.

"Have you made a decision?" Mikael asks.

"Heal them and get out," the vampire replies.

I look up as he stands, staring at him as Cyril grudgingly begins to heal my body. Being healed hurts as much as the initial harm, everything stitching itself back together and righting broken or fractured bones, but I don't look away from the vampire. He walks around the room slowly, allowing Dorian and I both glimpses of him. Dorian glares as he leans away from Cyril's healing touch, then sits stiffly when we're left alone with the vampire. The man stands directly behind Dorian's chair, running a hand idly through his hair. Dorian stares at me, fear in every line of his body as his head is tilted to the side and long hair pulled away from his neck. The vampire licks a stripe up his neck, humming in pleasure at the blood that coats Dorian's skin still. Dorian shudders with revulsion.

Then the vampire bites down.

"*Stop,*" I beg as Dorian whimpers quietly. The vampire continues drinking his blood. Dorian shivers and squeezes his eyes shut, jaw clenched. "*Please!* Just let him go."

"Ah, only so I can have a taste of both of you," the vampire says, wiping blood away from his lip as he straightens. The gesture is so unnervingly like Armel's after he bit me that I shudder. Dorian leans away from the vampire, breathing shakily as he grips the chair tightly.

The vampire approaches me. "What do you *want?*" I ask.

"You," he answers. "Or your darling brother." He stops in front of me, grinning. "A little fun with Mikael."

"You have a fucked up sense of fun," I say, leaning away as he reaches for me. His nails are long, expertly tended to and painted blood red. He caresses my cheek—then the points of his nails, almost talons, dig into my cheeks as he grips my face and holds my head still.

"It hurts more when you move," he says softly.

He tilts my head back, breath ghosting across my skin as he lowers his head. He doesn't lick as he did with Dorian, just bites down. I stare at the ceiling—pain and pleasure radiate out from his bite, a feeling that makes warmth curl throughout my body as the pleasure overcomes the pain. He sucks gently. I gasp.

"The fay-touched are always so much sweeter," he whispers in my ear. "But I can smell Armel on you. It ruins you."

He turns my head to look into my eyes, smiling as he runs his finger over my lips. I spit in his face. "Go fuck yourself."

His nails dig into my cheek, lines of pain erupting as he drags them down. Blood drips into my mouth. "Pity to ruin that pretty face of yours."

I glare at him as he steps away. He smiles back, revealing his fangs, then turns to Dorian again. Dorian stares back, jerking away when the vampire comes close. Again, he stands behind Dorian. Dorian squeezes his eyes shut, but the vampire meets my gaze as he uses one nail to slice his own wrist. Blood drips down his arm as he brings his wrist to Dorian's mouth. Dorian's eyes fly open as he tries to lean away, but the vampire holds him steady. Forces him to swallow the blood in his mouth. Dorian grips the chair tightly again as the vampire places his hands on Dorian's shoulders and leans down to place his mouth over his previous bite. He sucks and Dorian flinches.

And ever so slowly, Dorian relaxes. I tug at my ropes again as his head droops forward, but they have no give and I remain tied to the chair. When the vampire finishes and straightens, I don't know who to stare at—the vampire or my brother, his breathing evening out into nothing. The vampire wipes his mouth daintily with a kerchief as he stares at me, dark eyes alight with amusement. I watch him warily as he comes to me again, wishing I could at least kick him as he stands behind my chair.

"Should I do the same to you? Set you both free to drink your fill of Mikael and his men?" he asks, pulling my hair back as he tilts my head to the side. Dorian doesn't move, chest too still. His hair covers his face as it had before he'd woken. The vampire's breath ghosts across my ear. "Would you like that? Taking your revenge on him?"

I shudder and shake my head, tears falling down my cheeks.

He chuckles, running his finger along the scratches he dug into my cheek. I lean away, but his other hand falls to my shoulder to pin me in place. "No," he says. "I think I'll just change your brother. What *will* they say of the Bellerose boys amongst the fay now, I wonder?"

That we were fools who knew better, I think as he sucks on his bite again.

The same mixture of pain and pleasure again, the pain ebbing away to be replaced by pure pleasure, a lightness that pulls me under until black overcomes my vision.

THREE

J oss."

I groan softly.

"*Joss.*"

I open my eyes slowly, staring at the blood that covers my body. A perfectly good linen shirt absolutely ruined—stiff and sticky with blood, slashed into ribbons from Cyril's blade. Not important, though. Important is the way Dorian breathes heavily, how he tries to hide a whimper. I look up. He clutches at his chair, body braced against the pain wracking his body. His eyes are squeezed shut, jaw clenched as he lets out a harsh breath. He's covered in as much blood as I am, but none of it is new. Mikael and Cyril haven't returned to us and gone back to work on our bodies while I've been unconscious.

The vampire has left, though.

"What happens next?" Dorian asks.

I twist, trying to look behind me. Nothing, no one, just the torches that line the walls.

I can move my wrist more than I could before.

I look down, examining the soaked and fraying rope around my right wrist.

"*Joss,*" Dorian says, almost a whine. It reminds me of when we were younger, the same tone he'd take before we'd found our footing amongst the fay, the tone he had because I was older and I had all the answers to him.

Terrifies me to hear that tone from him right now. "You're fine," I say, rubbing the rope against the edge of the armrest.

"Are you *really* lying to me right now?" he asks.

I glance up at him through the hair that's fallen in front of my face, grinning until I see his face. He looks so *pale,* dark circles around his eyes like he hasn't slept in days. I doubt I look much better, but at least I don't have the pain of a vampiric transformation coursing through my body. There's a tooth next to his foot from where one of his fangs grew in and forced it out. A fledgling vampire should have their sire with them to soothe them through the transformation, but Dorian has to go through it alone and tied up because of me.

"You'll *be* fine," I amend, twisting my wrist to see if I can slip my hand under the rope. It's still too tight for that, but it's still fraying. A little more and I can get free. I keep going. "I'm going to get you out of here. I promise. And then we'll find help."

"Help like you found when you needed money?"

I wince. "I'll take you to Armel."

He almost laughs, but it becomes a shuddering, hitching gasp as his back arches from the pain. "At least," he starts, before he pauses to breathe. "At least you're going to be smart *now*."

"Better than going to Malo or Maiwenn," I mutter.

His head falls forward again. I watch him as I tug on the rope. He's still breathing too heavily, still gripping the chair too tightly, still too damn pale. The wood cracks under one of his hands, startling him right before another wave of pain overwhelms him. When this one passes, he spits out another tooth and a mouthful of blood. I grimace as the tooth bounces against his leg, then falls to the floor.

"*Fuck*," he breathes out. "No one says it hurts this much."

The rope snaps. I laugh triumphantly, shaking out my hand. Dorian looks up with a frown, then his eyes widen when he sees my hand.

"Joss," he says. "*Joss.* The rope was fine before."

"I know," I reply, tugging on the rope around my other wrist.

"That means—"

"I *know*. The vampire wants to have more *fun*." I look at him as I pick at the knot. "I know how to summon Armel, though. He taught me after he hired me and there's enough fucking blood here to use for it."

He nods. "Do you really think he can help?"

"He's the best option," I say, freeing my wrist. I rub my wrists gently, flinching at how raw they feel, then bend over to remove the rope around my ankles.

Dorian stops speaking, but he doesn't fall entirely silent. Not with the pain he's in. I listen to his breathing as I unravel the knots and toss the rope aside, grimacing as I examine how the skin around my ankles looks. Bad, could be worse, but not so terrible that I can't move. I stand slowly, holding onto the chair until I'm sure I won't fall over, then throw myself at Dorian. He wears an absolutely miserable expression, watching as I kneel to start picking at the knot of the rope around his left wrist.

I nearly have it until the rope suddenly tightens again, making Dorian gasp from the pain. I spin at the magic, slipping in congealed blood and wishing I'd grabbed a tool off the table as Mikael advances on me. He's between me and the table, long strides easily closing the distance between us and he's hitting me before I can even stand. I slip on the blood again, landing hard on my hip and shoulder. Mikael kicks me in the stomach, then hauls me to my knees.

"Did you think you could *run?*" he asks. "Off my estate, without anyone seeing you? We're not even in the City anymore."

Fuck.

Dorian and I exchange alarmed looks before Mikael shakes me.

"We're not *done,*" he hisses, throwing me at my chair.

I turn my head aside and throw a hand up, knocking the chair over as I land. One of the legs slams into my ribs and I grit my teeth against the impact, looking back at Mikael. Behind him, Cyril turns away from the table with a coil of fresh rope. Dorian tugs at his ropes again, then hisses in pain as they tighten—before gasping and gripping the armrests as a fresh wave of pain from his vampiric transformation burns through him, making him double over. Mikael stares at him, then laughs.

"Oh, that's *perfect,*" he says, lifting Dorian's head. Dorian glares at him, but Mikael looks at me. "You fucked up so badly you got your baby brother turned into a vampire."

I stare back as impassively as I can, refusing to show just how deep that cuts. Cyril grabs my arm, pulling me to my feet as he rights the chair. I'm shoved into the chair, Cyril waving a hand at the rope. It breaks into four pieces—but before it can cut through the air and wrap around me, a torch on the wall flickers, then gutters out entirely. A corner of the room falls into darkness. Mikael and Cyril both step back, staring at it.

The thing that comes out of the shadows is not human.

It might look human in lower light—but not here, not now, with other torches still illuminating the room. There's no hair on its head, slight bumps and small holes where ears should be. Its round eyes are completely white, pupil-less as it looks around the room. And it *looks*, staring directly at me before glancing at Dorian, then fixing its attention on Mikael and Cyril. It has no nose, just slits in its face under its eyes, but those slits flare as it inhales. It crawls forward, skeletal body too long. Too *wrong*. I shudder as I lean away, but I can't *look* away. Its crawl is more akin to a skitter, head tilting to the side as it approaches. Its skin is bleached bone white, and when it grins, its mouth is as red as the blood under me and it has too many teeth. Jagged, sharp teeth, used to tear meat apart.

It stops next to me, looking at me again before reaching out. I flinch away—its fingers are too long, too many joints.

It focuses on Mikael again.

Mikael stumbles back, cursing and demanding Cyril *do* something. Cyril attempts some magic, but the creature waves its hand to ward off the attack. It stands slowly, too tall for the room as it hunches over and continues to advance on them. Mikael falls against the wall and paws at the door as he stares up into the creature's face, but the creature slams the door shut when he manages to get it open. It grins again, letting out a wheezing noise that almost sounds like a laugh. Cyril lunges for his tools, but the creature is too fast, too long. It grabs

Cyril's ankle, squeezing tight enough Cyril grunts in pain. He scrabbles for something—to hold, use as a weapon—as he's pulled back but the creature is quickly on him and biting into his neck.

Cyril doesn't get a chance to make a noise. He barely twitches.

The creature turns its attention on Mikael again. Mikael backs into a corner, shaking his head as the creature gets close enough Mikael's nose presses against the flat expanse of face where the creature's nose should be.

I don't know if I can watch it bite Mikael's *face* off.

I throw myself at Dorian's chair, clawing at the ropes to free him. He falls forward into my arms with a whimper, tensed against another wave of pain wracking his body. "It's okay," I tell him as he finally lets out a sob. "I'm going to get us out of here."

"You're going to get yourself *killed,*" Nikolay snaps. He yanks Dorian away from me, forcing him to look him in the eye. "*Sleep,* Dorian Bellerose of the ash. Feel no more pain." Dorian's eyes close as he goes limp, his breathing evening out. Nikolay sets him down gently, then scowls at me. I stare at him. He's completely naked and covered in blood, a trail that starts at his mouth like he's had a particularly messy meal. I try not to look at Cyril's corpse. Nikolay grabs my face with one hand, squishing my cheeks and shaking my head lightly. "What is *wrong* with you?"

"That was you," I say softly. "What the fuck are you?" Then his question hits me and I frown. "Nothing's wrong with me!"

"A *fledgling*," he hisses. "And you put his fucking mouth right next to your throat!"

"He's my *brother*," I snap, shoving his hand away. He scoffs, falling back when I shove him away from Dorian. "What did you do to him?"

"Exactly what I said," Nikolay answers. "He's asleep, and he's not feeling any pain."

I glance up at him, relief and indignation warring within me. "How long will it last?"

"As long as I want."

"Can you keep him asleep for the entire transformation?"

His stare is a hard one. "Yes, but I won't. I'll keep him asleep until we get him to a vampire who can help, and then she'll ask him what he wants to do."

I nod, brushing Dorian's hair away from his face. "What are you then?"

"A mare," Armel says behind me. "They make *excellent* hunters."

I stare at Nikolay anew. *That's* the predator to him, the way he got into the heads of everyone in the City. He got into people's *dreams,* their nightmares, and it took *one fucking night.* An entire fucking city in one fucking night.

Nikolay stares back silently as Armel walks past us to crouch in front of a whimpering Mikael. "Mikael Trahan, son of Padrig Trahan and Béatrice Faucher," he says softly. "I've tolerated you for long enough. You'll not come near Jocelyn Bellerose of the ash again. You'll not come near his brother. Do you understand?" Mikael nods, but Armel grabs his face and moves closer. I can't see his expression, but the fear on Mikael's face and the spreading wet stain of him pissing himself is enough. "Do you understand who you've made enemies of? What will happen to you?"

Mikael nods and whimpers.

"Good," Armel says as he stands. He turns to look at me.

I speak before he can. "Did you knowingly send me after a fucking *mare?*"

He smiles as he walks over. "No. I didn't know he was a mare until we'd realized you'd been taken by Mikael. Then I hired him to find you." He crouches when he reaches us, taking my chin in his hand as he looks me over. "Let's get you out of here, pet."

I nod and let him help me to my feet, but then he lifts me into his arms. Nikolay takes my brother, carrying him into the shadows. I rest my head against Armel's shoulder as he follows Nikolay, closing my eyes as we step into the shadows and between the realms. A heartbeat of cold before a comfortable warmth surrounds us, and I open my eyes to look around an unfamiliar sitting room. The decor *reeks* of Armel's tastes, though—dark browns with reds and creams, stripes and solids against figures carved into dark wood, animals who prance around trees and humans writhing in ecstasy. A fox darts under a couch to watch us. Another is sprawled across a footstool, ears twitching in its sleep when we arrive.

Armel nods for Nikolay to follow him. He leads him down a hallway, stopping at a room with a window in the door to direct Nikolay to put Dorian in there. I expect him to put me down then, but he carries me farther down the hallway and upstairs instead, where a door opens on its own to reveal a large bedroom. I clutch his shoulders a little tighter, staring at the room with wide eyes—but I can't tell if it's a room he uses regularly or not. Either way, he sets me down just within the doorway and takes my face in his hands.

"When you're ready for me to heal any injuries, tell me," he says.

"Now," I reply. "But I don't know where the injuries are. You could help me look."

His thumb moves across my cheek. "We need to get the blood off you first."

I nod, sighing and closing my eyes. "You could help with that, too." I open my eyes, glancing around the room. "I thought you lived above the club."

"Some nights," he says, moving up against my side. He lifts one hand, sketching a sigil in the air as he kisses my temple. "Other nights I'm here."

"Oh," I whisper, leaning against him—then I see his cloak and silk shirt stained with my blood. I grimace and lean away, pulling the tattered remains of my shirt away from my body. "Where's the bath?"

"Through here," he answers, lifting me into his arms again.

I protest, but he shushes me quickly as he walks through the doorway he's summoned and into a small grove. Foxes dance and yip around us as he carries me to the door of a cottage, but they stay outside when we enter it. The room is warm, a fire crackling in the hearth and a large tub of steaming water in the corner. Armel carries me over to the tub and sets me down next to it, sighing lightly as he reaches for my shirt. He goes gently, the shirt sticking to dried blood in a few spots, then kneels in front of me to help me out of my boots. He pushes my trousers down gently after, tossing them aside before running his hands along the backs of my legs as he reaches for my underclothes. I step out of those with a sigh, rubbing my neck as I step back towards the tub. He stands and helps me into it, but I don't let him go once I'm in the warm water. I unclasp his cloak instead, pushing it off his shoulders.

"You can't heal anything from over there," I say as I step back. I lower myself into the water, sitting against the far edge of the tub as I stare at him.

He smiles and undresses, pinning his long hair up as he steps into the tub. I don't pretend to look anywhere else but at him. His entire body is thick with muscle, scarred from past battles; his nipples are pierced with plain silver bars today and a light dusting of hair over his chest leads down to his cock, but he's sitting next to me and taking my hands in his before I can look too much. He's gentle, rubbing the blood from my skin, but I still flinch when his hands move over my wrists. He clicks his tongue as he lifts my hands, examining my wrists and the damage done by the ropes. I sit still as he works on one wrist and then the other, rubbing magic into them gently to heal the damage away until not even a scar remains.

What he thinks about all the blood and remaining injuries, he doesn't say. I let him move me around as we wipe the blood from me and he heals the injuries. My cheek where the vampire dug his nails into my skin comes last, Armel frowning as he holds his hand over my face. I close my eyes as my face warms from the magic, the skin knitting itself back together. His healing magic is slow, near painless, the same gentleness he's had since we first met. After my face is healed, Armel wipes the blood away and helps me get the blood from my hair.

I open my eyes when he pulls away from me. He holds his hand above the water, pulling the blood from it to form a small orb beneath his palm that hardens into a dark pearl. He examines the pearl, then sets it aside. "That will be nice to have," he says.

I dunk my head again, frowning when I sit up. "What about my debt?" I ask. "You told Mikael to never come near me again, but he still holds my debt."

"I bought your debt from the family." I stare at him. I got through years of living with the fay without owing them anything, and now he does this. He lowers himself in the water, moving closer slowly. I back up until I hit the edge of the tub. He pushes my legs apart gently, then runs his hands along my legs as he moves between them. "I said I would leave Mikael alive if they gave it to me."

"Any chance I could persuade you to forgive it?"

He smiles, looking at me from under lowered lashes. "It's possible. You want to discuss this now?"

"If I let you fuck me, will you forgive it?"

He chuckles and kisses my collarbone before whispering in my ear. "From you, all I'd need is the promise of a favor in the future."

I place my hands against his arms, tilting my head back. "Can I pick the favor?"

He's silent for a moment, pulling me completely into his lap. "No," he says, arms around my waist as he stands with me in his arms. "You have to accept the first favor I ask of you."

Dangerous.

I cling to him as he carries me from the tub and over to the fire, where he sets me down on top of a thick blanket. He hovers over me, still between my legs. "How long did Mikael have us?" I ask quietly.

"A little more than a day," he answers. I nod, running my fingers over his chest. He lowers himself, hips pressing against me, and kisses my neck. Where the vampire bit me.

I squirm away from him, then direct his mouth to mine before he can question me. "Yes," I tell him as I kiss him. "Forgive my debt and I'll owe you one favor."

"We have a bargain."

I nod, wrapping my legs around his waist. "Are you still going to try fucking me?"

His cock rubs against me as he smiles. "Do you want me to?"

I bite my lip as I consider, then nod and kiss him again. His long body stretches out along mine, and he kisses me slowly, deeply. One hand holds my face as the other moves down along my chest, teasing until I can squirm enough to allow his hand to slip between my legs, fingers sliding against me easily.

And then a fox starts yipping outside the cottage, others following it.

Armel sighs, pushing up onto his knees as he looks at the door. I lay back, letting my arms rest over my head. He cocks his head to the side as if listening to something, then shakes his head. "We need to return."

"I should go home," I say, sitting up and pulling my legs against my chest. "Unless Mikael destroyed it." I rest my cheek against my knee and stare at the fire. So much to do.

"He didn't, and you don't have to," Armel says as he stands. I lift my head to watch him as he walks over to a small wardrobe and pulls out fresh clothing as he beckons for me.

"I can stay here?" I ask, gesturing to the cottage as I stand.

He shakes his head as I walk over. "No," he says, passing me a pair of trousers and a simple linen shirt. "This is merely a piece of a realm I stole. You don't want to be here without me to control it."

"Good to know," I murmur, glancing around.

He lifts me into his arms again once we're dressed, carrying me from the cottage. The foxes prance around him again as he walks through the grove, but he pays them no mind and summons a doorway to return us to his home. I'm set down in the same bedroom as before, Armel tucking my hair behind an ear before he steps away.

"The vampires are here," he says. "I have to see what they need. But this room is yours for however long you need it."

I nod, standing in the middle of the room as he leaves. A noise makes me jump and whip around, but it's only a fox laying on the bed. Its tail twitches as we look at each other. I take a step forward and it scuttles across the bed, ready to play—then darts under the bed with such speed that I jump back. It chitters at me. I sigh, running a hand over my face.

Safe.

I'm safe here. Dorian's safe here. That's all that matters.

FOUR

I FEEL LIKE A ghost wandering Armel's manor, and I avoid the two vampires that come to help Dorian through his transformation. They speak only to Armel once Nikolay leaves, and when I peek through the window into the room that's become Dorian's prison, they glance at me but never say anything. Once, though, the woman shakes her head at me and gestures for me to go as she mouths *not yet.* Dorian sits hunched over then, head in his hands and body trembling. I sit by the door for a bit before I leave them to find another place to haunt.

Nikolay returns while I explore Armel's library, stepping out of the shadows and coming up behind me. I don't turn around immediately, unsure of what will greet me—monster or human guise—but curiosity draws me into turning. He stands there in his human guise, damp hair pushed back from his face, clothes tailored to the sharp edges of his body. I don't know what to do with the disappointment that pokes at me, so I poke at him instead, tugging on the neckline of his shirt. He looks far less *serious* here, not one of Yves Chastain's men. He looks alive, blood pumping through his body and giving warmth to his pale skin. He has ears and a nose, his eyes dark and warm. He's still tall, still thin, not as tall and thin as he was before. He's barefoot, too.

He grows amused at the way I poke and stare at him without saying anything. "Armel said he was keeping you locked up," he says.

I step closer, opening his shirt as I look at his chest. There are ways to know when a body is only a construct, but I can't feel anything strange when I run my hand over his chest. "I'm not allowed to leave until things settle," I say, wrinkling my nose up as I remember that argument. "He's feeling protective."

"Unsurprising. Are you done fondling my chest?"

"No," I say, and I put both hands on his chest, spreading my fingers wide and squeezing gently as I grin at him. He rolls his eyes. "Is that what you really look like? What I saw before?" He nods. "Can I see it again?"

"No." He tilts his head, watching as I move my hands down to his stomach. "Are you avoiding your brother?"

It's like being doused in ice-cold water.

I pull my hands away and step back, shaking my head as I return to the bookshelf I'd been perusing. "He's still wracked by pain," I say softly. "That will take a little longer to ease—but he also needs to focus on what they can teach him. Not see me and remember whose fault it is he's now a vampire." I tug on the spine of a book without pulling it out, swallowing thickly. "He'll need to find somewhere to live. Maiwenn won't let a vampire through her door."

"Maiwenn?" Nikolay asks, stepping close enough his breath ghosts across the back of my neck.

"She took us in when we were children," I explain. "Fay, like Armel, but lesser blood. She was terrible at raising children."

"Most fay are. They don't have children very often." I nod. He reaches past me, pulling out the book my hand rests on. A collection of ballads. "Dorian will be able to stay with Alana until he can support himself."

"Oh," I whisper. "That's good."

"It's Mikael's fault he's now a vampire."

I twist to frown at him. "Mikael kidnapped him because of *me*. That vampire was there because of *me*."

"Still not your fault." He pauses, looking from the ballads to me slowly. "Tell me about the vampire."

I shake my head. "He was fay, but I didn't recognize him. He's new to the City if he lives here. And yes, my fault—all of this happened because I took out a loan with Mikael." I sidle by Nikolay, stepping away from the bookshelf—but I don't know where to go or what to do.

"I doubt Dorian blames you," he says, putting the ballads back on the shelf. He steps up to me, pushing my hair behind an ear as he tilts my face up towards his. I wait to see what he wants.

And then a fox darts across the room, bumping into a table and rattling everything on it.

I startle and jump forward into Nikolay's chest, gripping his arms tightly. "Fucking *foxes*," I hiss. "They're everywhere. Armel is *not* keeping me here."

"The Trahan family will go after you again," Nikolay says. "It's better to stay here."

"There are rooms above the club. I can stay there."

"The club isn't protected like this place is."

I glare at him. He stares back impassively. It's like seeing him in the club while he had two fingers buried in me again, and it makes my irritation spike. I step away, glaring at the fox who peeks out from under a couch. "Get out," I snap at it. It doesn't move. I storm over to the library door, yanking it open before I turn to the couch. The fox darts out from under it, hesitating in the middle of the room until Nikolay steps towards it, then runs out the door. I slam it shut behind the fox and spin around to glare at Nikolay again.

He doesn't move, doesn't look away from me. I don't think as I walk over to him. I don't *want* to think. I want to forget about Mikael torturing me for hours. I want to forget about the vampire's smile as he forcibly turned my brother. I want to forget about the pain Dorian is going through because of me. I want to forget about the favor I now owe Armel. Just for a moment, I want to forget.

I pull Nikolay down to me and kiss him. He immediately pulls me against his body, deepening the kiss. I shove his shirt off, then shove at his trousers. He lets me undress him, keeps kissing me with his hands cradling my face, and I expect him to start undressing me when one of his hands starts moving down my body. But he doesn't, just turns us towards the bookshelf and backs me up against it as his hand slips into my trousers to rub two fingers against me. I groan, digging my nails into his shoulders as I move against his fingers.

It's not enough, just his fingers. I shove my trousers off and he's on his knees, lifting my leg over his shoulder, before I can do much else. I grip the shelf as he runs his tongue over me, then slips one finger into me. He looks up as he sucks gently. I nearly buckle there—a fucking mare on his knees with his mouth against my clit. He pulls back enough to let me see his smirk, then puts his mouth against me again and pushes a second finger in before I can say anything. I grab a fistful of his hair and hold him in place, digging the heel of my foot into his back as I moan and move against his tongue. He adjusts the way he kneels, curling his fingers as he thrusts them. I bite my lip, then gasp when he sucks harder. My hips rock down, and I shudder when my orgasm hits me. He's a menace, stroking and sucking me through it until I'm shoving him away and sliding to the floor as I suck in a deep breath. He wipes his chin off as I glance at his cock—hard between his legs, pleasantly thick and long.

"Couch," I order. "I'm not getting fucked on the floor."

He closes the distance between us to place a soft kiss against my neck. "No?"

I shove him away. "No," I say, crawling towards the couch. He grabs my hips and pulls me back, running his tongue along my cunt again before pushing it in. I drop my head onto the floor with a quiet whine as he fucks me with his tongue. "*Fuck.* Maybe—*no.* No! On the floor hurts."

He laughs and lets me go. I get unsteadily to my feet and run for the couch. Nikolay is on me almost immediately, grabbing fistfuls of my shirt and pulling me back against him. "Don't run from mares," he whispers, pushing my legs apart as I'm placed on the couch and bent over the back of it. He kneels between my legs, teasing me with his cock before pushing it in. I bite my lip to hold back a moan, gripping the couch tightly. He goes slow, but he doesn't stop until his cock's entirely buried.

"If running means I get your cock in me, I'm afraid I'll run *a lot,*" I tell him, glancing over my shoulder.

He tilts my head back to kiss me. "And *that* is why I won't be showing you my true form again."

"But I want to—"

He pulls back—then thrusts hard enough the couch rocks. I let out a nervous giggle, fingers flexing against the back of the couch. He hums, kissing the spot under my ear as he starts a slow rhythm with his hips. None of the force of that first thrust, but it's enough to know it's there, that he could use that strength again—and has me wondering what his strength is like when he's in his true form as a mare. He holds one hand against my neck, keeping my head tilted back, and pushes me forward so he can grab the back of the couch as he moves, as he picks up speed. I open my legs farther, as much as I'm able, letting go of the couch so I can reach down and touch myself.

He *growls* at that.

I freeze, not entirely sure what that's supposed to mean. He nips at my ear, dropping his hand from my neck to guide my hand back to my clit. "Don't stop," he whispers.

I shiver and nod as he kisses me. He keeps his hand over mine, guiding me into touching his cock as it moves. I squeeze the base of it, just to see what happens, and get a bite on my shoulder in return. My laugh turns into a moan as his fingers move to my clit and begin to rub against it. He covers my mouth with his other hand, then hisses when I bite his palm.

"You and your *biting*," he says.

"You just bit me! Fair's fair," I retort.

He tilts my head back again to stare at me, judging something, before moving us to lay me out across the couch on my back. "*No biting*," he says as he slips two fingers into my mouth and his cock back into me. I moan instead, nodding. "Hands up there," he adds, pointing to the armrest. I glare but hold onto it. "Good," he murmurs, kissing my collarbone. "That's my boy."

It is *terrible* how much I'd do to hear him say that again.

As it is, I wrap my legs around his hips to push him deep and suck on his fingers as he presses them down against my tongue. He hovers over me, hand gripping the couch cushion under my head. Here, at this angle, he picks up speed, hips snapping forward, and uses enough force I hear the couch tremble again. I moan around his fingers and forget his order to keep my hands up, grabbing at him and dragging my nails down his back. He shudders, and pulls his fingers from my mouth to rub at my clit again. I arch under him, shuddering and biting my lip until he licks up my neck to kiss me again.

When I climax, he's hovering above me, watching. His fingers don't stop, nor do his hips, not until I dig my nails in and hold him still against me. I stare up at the ceiling and tremble as he ducks his head down to kiss my shoulder, then wrap my arms around him lightly, running my fingers through his hair. He rocks his hips gently.

I glance at the side of his head. "Did you—"

"No."

"Oh."

He lifts himself up and pulls his cock out slowly, smiling at how I squirm before he pries my legs free of him. "Roll over," he orders, moving my legs before

I can even process what he's said. I scoff, but roll over to lay on my stomach, stretching my arms out. Immediately, he's on top of me, holding my hands down above my head. "Lift your hips."

"Are you going to call me good again?" I ask, wiggling to do what he wants. I can feel his cock against my ass and I want to feel it *in* me again.

There's a long pause before he answers, long enough the back of my neck starts to burn from embarrassment. "Do you want me to?" he asks eventually. I hide my face against the couch, but he's relentless. He pulls my hair back with one hand, licking the shell of my ear and blowing gently. I startle and try to squirm away, but his other hand holds both of my wrists and his weight above me keeps me from going anywhere. "Is that what you like? Getting ordered about and praised?"

"*No,*" I say, too fast and too high. I can feel his grin against my neck. "Shut up and fuck me," I snap.

He wastes no time, shoving his cock in quickly. "I'd tell you to keep your hands there, but I don't think I trust you to do so."

"Shame you have no rope," I reply.

He chuckles as he thrusts with a hard pace that has me forgetting how to speak almost immediately. "Do you like *that*, too? Ordered around, praised, tied up . . ." He trails off, but I don't get the chance to speak with the way he fucks me, nor with the way he puts two fingers in my mouth again as he whispers in my ear. "Gagged, too?" Shadows curl around the couch like tentacles, reaching to hold my hands down. I stare as they slide along my skin, cold but not too tight as they wrap around my wrists and free his hand. "I could tie you up in my office and make you wait while I work."

His shadows curl and undulate along my wrists, never staying in one spot for too long. Nikolay kisses my shoulder, moving his fingers along my tongue. I moan around his fingers, eyes fluttering shut.

"Would you like that?" he asks softly. I nod—I don't think I'd mind being tied up and forced to wait for him. "Then be a good boy, Joss, and we'll see what we can do together."

My third orgasm comes too quickly.

Nikolay laughs and lifts himself up, taking his fingers from my mouth and holding onto my hips as he fucks me through my orgasm, unrelenting until he reaches his own climax and buries his cock deep before he goes still. A thin tendril of a shadow teases my lips and I bite at it as Nikolay slowly pulls his cock from me. He bats the shadow away as he sprawls half on top of me, and the shadow recedes with the ones around my wrists. I lift my hands, examining my wrists—no bruises, nothing to hide. No repeat of the damage done by Mikael.

I look over at Nikolay. He watches me through half-open eyes. His hair's a mess, a light sheen of sweat covering him, and he looks so human I could easily forget that he's a mare. I push myself up, ignoring the way my legs tremble and tugging on his arm until he's laying under me and I can drop on top of him. He snorts, but he starts toying with my hair as I rest my cheek against my hand.

"What was that?" I ask.

"That was you pouncing on me," he says, before pulling me to him for a slow, sweet kiss. "And you needed a distraction."

"Oh," I whisper, smiling slowly. "I needed a distraction."

"Are you going to argue with me?"

I shake my head, unable to stop smiling. "No." I bite my lip, then lean forward to kiss him again. "But I still want to see your true form."

He stares at me for a moment before shaking his head. I pout, but he silences me with another kiss, rolling us over slowly to pin me under him again. "No," he says against my mouth. "You're human, Joss. It's too dangerous."

I roll my eyes. "We'll work up to it." He shakes his head again, but there's a smile tugging at his lips. "In the meantime," I add, "you can answer all my questions about being a mare."

His smile grows, his thumb running along my lower lip. "Another time. I'm already late for an appointment with Yves."

I grin as he stands and dresses. "I made you late? Nikolay Voronin is never late! You're always there first. One of Yves's brothers brags about it."

He glances at me over his shoulder as he steps into a doorway of shadows not unlike the doorway to Armel's pocket realm. I stay on the couch and watch the space where he disappeared, unsure about trusting my legs to carry me out of the library. I should go, though, and check on Dorian. He needs me as much as he needs the vampires, and he'll need me more than anyone when Maiwenn learns what happened. I sigh and roll off the couch, pulling on my abandoned clothes. I examine my shirt as I leave the library, but it looks fine for having had sex in it.

The hallway is empty when I step into it and I creep down it, listening to the manor's noises. Foxes somewhere, but no voices carry to me. I slip into my room for a coat and pair of boots before walking downstairs to Dorian's room, and I glance at the door as I set my boots and coat aside.

The clatter of something being thrown against a wall makes me jerk upright and look through the window.

One of the vampires is there—the man, sea-blue eyes trained on Dorian. He stands in a corner with his arms crossed and only watches the tantrum Dorian seems to be throwing. Dorian paces, kicks at a chair, snaps something at the other vampire. The vampire shrugs in response. Dorian kicks the chair towards him. Another chair lies shattered against the wall. I can't hear what they're saying, but I can see the rage in every line of Dorian's body, how it grows when the vampire doesn't rise to the bait. Not everyone is as hot-headed and easy to bait as Malo.

The vampire glances at me. He nods.

I open the door and step into the room. Dorian spins around, almost slumping forward when he sees me and relaxes. I give the broken chair a pointed look. He looks over, winces as he looks away. The vampire leaves the corner, whispering something to Dorian as he passes him. There are no words for me as I step aside to allow him to leave. I stare at the window, but he doesn't stand by it to watch us.

"Are you all right?" Dorian asks.

"I should be asking you that," I answer as I walk into the room and right the kicked chair. Dorian glances at me as I sit in it, then sits on the floor in front of me and stares at his hands in his lap. I abandon the chair to sit next to him. "Is it easier with them?"

He nods. "Alana is the head of their clan. She knows what she's doing." He sighs, sitting up and looking around the room. "What do we do now? Mikael's not a threat anymore."

"I'm going to go visit Armel at the club and discuss just that," I say.

Dorian's head whips around. "What?"

I shrug. "Mikael's not a threat, and there's too many foxes here."

"You can't just *leave*."

"I'll come back," I say. "An hour or two, that's all." He starts to protest again and I shake my head. "If I talk to Armel, we can make a plan for what happens when we tell Maiwenn about you being a vampire now."

He grimaces. "I hadn't thought of that."

"Hopefully she takes it better than when I left." His laugh is humorless. I try to smile for him. "She will. You were always her favorite." He sighs and nods, looking down at his hands again. "Will you be all right if I go?" I ask him quietly.

He nods again, leaning over to hug me tightly. "Armel won't like it, though."

I laugh, hugging him back. "He can't complain. I won't leave his side once I'm there."

"Good," he says as he sits up.

I smile as I stand, kissing the top of his head before I leave him in that room again. He stays on the floor, watching me go, and the other vampire slips into the room as I leave. I collect my boots and coat, carrying them to the manor's front door, and tears threaten me as I struggle to pull my boots on. I manage, and yank the door open as I tug my coat on. What I need to do right now is help Dorian survive, and that means plans.

I walk down the street quickly, buttoning up my coat. I should've stolen one of Armel's cloaks with a hood. At least then I could better hide the way I wipe at tears as I navigate the Upper City, but I almost need not worry—no one approaches me, everyone too engrossed in each other and the errands that have dragged them out into the night. It makes walking to the club easier, albeit lonely.

My steps slow, then stop altogether when I turn a corner and see the lights of the club. The line in front of the doors is long, as it always is when Ryn is scheduled for the stage, and slow moving. I step back, leaning against a wall. I can almost hear Vola's jokes as people buy tickets from him. Sweet man. He starts whistling and shouting suddenly, and I strain to see why—then step back into the shadows of the building next to me when I see Armel walking along the line, Ryn right behind him. They each have a small bouquet of roses, pulling out flowers to give away as they decide who in the line has caught their eyes tonight. Ryn makes a beeline for the quietest, the ones who seem shy. He's sweet and gentle as he hands roses over to them, talking with one woman for a time before offering her a rose. Armel's at the end of the line before Ryn's even halfway, and Armel waves his last two roses as he turns to make his way back into the club.

I step forward, intent on joining him.

A hand takes my arm and pulls me back.

I spin, ready to shove whoever it is away, and they slap me hard enough I cut my cheek on my teeth. I spit the blood at them as I'm dragged down an alley and yank the hood of their cloak down. Petran Trahan glares at me. Mikael's younger brother. Surprise makes me slack. He shoves me up against a wall, forearm across my throat.

He slides a blade between my ribs.

I stare. Armel said—*he said they couldn't*—they wouldn't—

"You'll make it to the club," Petran snarls out. "You'll die in his arms. We had the blade charmed for that."

"Why?" I ask weakly. Such a stupid question. Does it matter?

"For Mikael," he says, twisting the blade before he removes it.

I slide to the ground, holding my hand against my chest as he drops the dagger and walks away. So easy for him to abandon me to die. I grit my teeth against the pain that tears through me as I get to my knees, then shakily to my feet. I kick the dagger away angrily, barely catching myself against the wall as I bite to my lip to keep from crying out. Charmed so I can die in *his* arms. Armel's, I'd wager, and Fate will weave itself around the charm to prevent escaping it. I take a moment—I let out one sob—then walk deeper into the alley.

I hope Armel kills them all.

But I won't show my fear as I walk to my death, navigating the alleys to find the club's back entrance. The door is propped open as it shouldn't be, and I kick at the block holding it open as I let myself inside. The door shuts softly behind me as I head to Armel's office, fumbling with the handle before I'm able to open it and slip in. His office is empty, but the spells he has on the room will have him here soon enough. I grab the open bottle of wine sitting on his desk as I walk by it, drinking deeply as I fall against the door to his boudoir. The door flies open against my weight, sending me crashing to the floor. The wine bottle hits my wound, knocking me breathless. When I crawl to the couch and heave myself onto it, I wheeze with the pain.

Fuck.

I don't know how long I lay there before I feel hands on my face. I open my eyes and stare into Armel's wide, amber ones. "Tell me you can do something," I whisper.

Nothing makes me want to cry more than the way he shakes his head. He lifts me as he sits on the couch, keeping me in his arms. "I told you to stay put," he murmurs, stroking my hair.

I hide my face against his neck, holding onto him weakly. "Sorry."

If he says anything, I don't hear it.

I stop feeling his arms around me.

I stop being able to hold onto him.

I take my last breath.

FIVE

Y OU DON'T EXPECT TO wake up after you die.

I stare at the sky beyond a canopy of trees.

Death comes for everyone, but the realms of the dead have never been something I considered much. Would I wake again? Would I not? Terrifying thoughts to hold in your head, and ones I found easier to bury than think about. And now I have to face the reality of *actually* waking up after dying. It might be a little more terrifying than anything else, simply because I cannot think of *why*. Why me? Why would I be given such a fate and not someone else, someone more worthy of that?

I close my eyes and take a deep breath, then open my eyes again.

It's not the forest Dorian and I grew up in. It's not Armel's pocket realm. It's not even the forest surrounding the City. It feels familiar, though—a little humid, smells a little bit like the sea. The air is sweetly cool in that space between winter and spring, just before dawn with the promise of a new day. I sit up slowly, staring down at the tunic, leggings, and boots I wear. Not what I'd been wearing, and not even what I'd once made Dorian promise to dress me in for my funeral were I to die before him. The ground under me is damp with dew, cold as I run my hand over it.

I look up.

A young man that I've never seen before sits in front of me. He looks my age, with the type of exhausted that doesn't quite go away. Doesn't look beaten down by it, though, staring at me with eyes that are two different colors—one a dark blue, the color of the deep sea, and the other silver as the moon. Three thin scars adorn the left side of his face, two of them bisected by his silver eye. His red hair is shoulder-length, braided along one side of his head and tucked behind pointed ears. Pale, fair, but not corpse white. Freckled from the sun. As I stare back, he slowly smiles and reveals deep dimples in his cheeks. "Hello," he says softly.

"Hello," I reply, leaning away. Don't trust strange people in the forest. Don't trust strange *fay* in the forest. It was one of the first lessons Maiwenn taught me and Dorian. "Who are you?"

He tilts his head to the side, glancing away as he thinks. "Somebody," he says slowly, focusing on me again as he toys with a sapphire earring.

"Somebody," I echo.

Behind me, someone snickers.

I turn to see a young, muscular woman leaning against a tree. Her green eyes are bright with merriment as she watches us, wrapping the end of a long braid around her fingers. "He's still figuring this out," she says with a grin.

"*Hush*," he says, then pauses. I glance at him, but he's giving the woman a slightly panicked look. ". . . you," he adds eventually. "Hush, you."

"Willow," she supplies.

He smiles. "*Hush*, Willow. He doesn't need to know that."

"I think I need to know that," I say, frowning. "Who are you? Both of you."

Willow saunters away from the tree, putting her hands on her hips when she reaches us and eyeing me. "Why him?" she asks, glancing at the redhead. "And you really need a name."

He waves a dismissive hand. "Later."

"All right. Why him?"

"I like him."

"And I like being ignored," I say loudly. "Thank you. It's all I've ever wanted."

She looks at him incredulously, but he's too busy grinning at me to notice. "*Somebody*," she says, "is a god."

He wrinkles his nose up at her. "You *agreed*."

"I changed my mind. He's *your* responsibility. Without me helping. Learn together."

"But—*Willow*—"

"No," she says, turning away from us and waving her hands around. "Your responsibility. *You* teach him to guide the dead."

"Guide the dead?" I repeat, before turning to stare at him. "*Guide the dead?*"

He grimaces. "I was supposed to tell you that with a very nice speech Willow made me learn."

"I—" I look for Willow, but she's already disappeared into the trees. When I turn back around, the young man is watching me warily. "You want me to be a fucking psychopomp?" He nods. I point to myself. "*Me?*"

He frowns. "Is that so hard to believe?"

I laugh far too loudly. "A little!" My laughter dies quickly and I drop my hands into my lap, shaking my head. "You don't even know me."

He shrugs. "I saw enough when you died." I wince. He sighs and stands, then takes my hands to pull me to my feet. He's a few inches shorter than me, and he looks up at me so sweetly, hints of his dimples in his cheeks. "Twenty-seven is young," he says. "Perhaps I want to give you another chance."

"At what?" I ask softly.

"Something. Anything." He shrugs and takes a step back, pulling me with him. "For now, come. We'll discover this together."

I shake my head again as I'm pulled along. "Who are you? She said you were a god. A god of what? I've never seen imagery of you before."

"The dead, the dying, Death. A few other things," he says, leading me through the trees to a cliff's edge where I can see the City. I frown, not recognizing this angle of it. This new god stands next to me, still holding my hand, and stares out at the City with me. "I'm merely an aspect. As are you now."

"What do I call you then?"

He sighs, loud and dramatic. It makes me smile. "I didn't think that far ahead," he says, lifting my hand and examining my palm. His sleeves fall back—constellations, feathers, and spiderwebs cover his forearms, looking almost like tattoos. "Kestrel," he adds, lowering our hands and shaking his sleeves back into place. "Call me Kestrel. And you're

Jocelyn Bellerose of the ash. Interesting sobriquet. What's it for?"

"Everyone calls me Joss," I correct. He nods. "And my brother and I were left by an ash tree."

"Left by an ash tree," he repeats, the question thick in his voice.

I nod. "By our parents." The rage flares to life in him, flashing across his face before he buries it—but it stays in his eyes. I smile a little and squeeze his hand. He squeezes back. "Why Kestrel?"

"One of my birds."

"And ravens?" I ask, lifting his hand and pulling his sleeve down to reveal the marks on his arms. Not quite tattoos—I know the look of ink on skin, and tattoos don't *move*. One constellation has winked out, feathers shifted to fill the space where it was. He inhales slowly, staring at my fingers as I trace the feathers. "Are those your birds as well?" He nods. "What else? What am I supposed to know about a god that's picked me?"

"I like holly," he says softly.

I look at the trees behind us, but he starts pulling me down a small trail along the cliffside. We have to let go of each other as we scramble down, rocks tumbling ahead of us. The path is an infrequently used one, Kestrel stopping once to let the land around us settle before he continues on. I study him as we descend to the water.

He fusses with his hair, poking at the braid and tucking his hair behind his ears again before he grows annoyed with that and shakes his head to free his hair again. The red shines with gold and silver under the sun, as bright against his fair skin as the sapphire and silver jewelry he wears. He toys with a necklace that disappears under his shirt, then toys with the neckline of his shirt and reveals more of those marks along his collarbones—branches and constellations twining together, a bird skull at the hollow of his throat.

At the water's edge, he stops to remove his boots and roll up his trousers before he marches into the water. I see a brief glimpse of another mark around his left leg—vines and thorns and poppies—and stare as he stands knee-deep in the water. The water swirls around the rocks here, little tide pools full of small crabs and other sea creatures. A cave opens in the cliffside, dark and forbidding even under a bright midday sun. Kestrel stares at it.

"What do you know of your City's history?" he asks abruptly.

"There were two here once," I answer as I remove my own boots. "One was swallowed by the sea ages ago."

He snorts. "It's so much easier to say the sea did it instead of your own people."

"War?" I ask as I follow him out into the water. He waits for me next to a large rock, holding a hand out as I get closer. I take his hand as I step around a tide pool, sticking my tongue out at a tiny crab that waves its claws at me.

"Perhaps," he answers, glancing back at the City. We can still see much of it from where we stand, and a ship waving a green flag leaves the harbor slowly. "I don't know exactly what happened, but magic is unpredictable like that. Whatever they did, though, forced the creation of a new realm." He frowns—at the City, at the sea, at the cave the water disappears into. "I've seen the void between realms and seen pieces of realms be lost to it, but your Cities . . . They weren't *lost*. They attached themselves like barnacles on a ship. And now one connects to the realm of the living, while the other is a City of the Dead. Shadows and reflections of each other," he murmurs. I frown as he looks at me, but he brightens into a smile quickly. "Do you want to see the other City?"

I nod. This was not a history Maiwenn taught me, and curiosity drives me on. Kestrel's smile grows and he gestures for me to follow him into the cave. The world quiets around us as we walk into it. He's short enough that the water reaches his waist at its highest, and he holds his boots up to keep them clear of the water. The water reaches my hips, soft sand under my feet. All I hear is water lapping against the edges of the cave, our soft breaths. It should be dark with the way we lose the sun, but as daylight recedes and darkness closes in, a soft glow starts under the water.

Rocks glow, some plants. Crystals in the walls. A soft blue light, almost violet, surrounds us and reflects onto the walls of the cave before the shadows above us swallow it. It's the most peaceful thing I've seen, my shoulders relaxing as I look around. Kestrel never stops leading me deeper, but he stops once when the cave walls around us light up like a night sky. He smiles and closes his eyes, bathed in the soft glow.

He looks like a god as he stands there, when he opens his eyes and looks back at me.

A god of the dead, of the dying, of Death—and something else. I can see it in his eyes as he gestures for me to follow him again. Kestrels are hunting birds, but ravens . . .

I grab his arm to stop him. He goes still, looking up at me. "Why me?" I ask. "What kind of god are you? What do you want with me?"

He twists his arm to free it, a slight smile on his lips, and runs his hand up the length of my arm. "I picked you because I liked you," he says, his fingers dancing along my shoulder to my neck. He runs his hand through my hair, then trails his fingers along my jaw. "I don't know what kind of god I am. Too many possibilities. But it's time I discover that, and I've decided I want to do that with you." His hand slides to the back of my neck and urges my head lower, low enough I think he might try to kiss me. That faint smile is still present as his thumb moves along my skin. "Would you come with me?" he asks softly. "Be my companion?"

I tilt my head to the side as I consider him, then quietly ask, "What do I do?"

"I don't know," he whispers back. "We'll learn together."

I smile a little. "You're a terribly unprepared god."

He laughs and tugs me lower to rest his brow against mine. "What do you say, Joss? Will you be my companion?"

I pretend to think about it a little longer, then nod. He kisses me then, pulling away slowly. At least death won't be *boring*.

"The only psychopomp I've dealt with is Willow, and she's not *mine*," he says as he starts leading me deeper into the cave again.

"I'm your first?" I ask with a silly grin.

He snorts. "You could say that. Now hush, we're almost there."

I fall silent, grin slowly fading as we continue on. The glow fades away as the water starts to lower, until we're sloshing through darkness with water around our knees. Light from the mouth of the cave comes to us slowly, the last bit of daylight after the sun sets. Kestrel stops at the mouth, one hand on a hip as he examines the land around us. The cave opens out onto the wide sea, tide pools and a cliff face surrounding it in a mirror image of the cave we entered.

Another City sits near us, this cave not so far from the harbor as the other. It looks much the same as my City, though the buildings here are dark and meld with the shadows around them. Torches hold a sickly green light to illuminate the streets, but the light doesn't look like it's nearly enough to illuminate the dark corners. Kestrel sloshes through the water to pull himself up onto some rocks, holding his arms out for balance as he walks towards a path lined with an ancient iron fence.

"The City of the Dead," he murmurs as I follow him. Then he frowns. "Oh."

I follow his gaze down the path to where it widens, a black coach waiting. A young man leans against it, chatting with the driver as they wait. "Are we expected?" I ask.

Kestrel glances at me. "Perhaps—but I've yet to meet Cú Lacha and sent no word to him."

"Who?"

"A revenant and a King of the Dead, the one who rules this City."

"Ah," I say softly. He nods. "How have you never met him? Revenants are the dead, and you're a god of the dead."

He shrugs. "He was here before I became this aspect of Death."

I open my mouth, then shut it. He keeps watching that coach—until my silence stretches on, and then he looks at me slowly, raising his brows. "Aspect of Death," I say. "You said something similar earlier. We're only aspects."

"Every realm, every culture, every *person*, has their own version of Death, their own psychopomp. I come to those who call to me, and so will you."

I nod despite not truly understanding and look to the coach. The man who leans against the side of it almost reminds me of Dorian—he has the same light, golden hair, the same posture with his back straight and arms crossed. The same bored expression. He's the opposite of the coach driver, even though the coach driver wears black from head to toe, hair as dark as his clothes but skin as pale as mine or Kestrel's. The other is just as pale, though it's not as striking with him as it is with the coach driver's dark clothes. His clothes are red and brown, trimmed with gold. "Who are they?" I ask Kestrel.

"I've no idea," he replies. "Shall we see?"

He's walking before I can reply. I stifle a sigh and follow, shaking my head. The path is packed dirt that clings to our wet feet and I glare at it, but Kestrel looks unbothered as he reaches the coach. The man leaning against the side steps forward and bows with a flourish, hand resting against the sword at his hip.

"Who are you?" Kestrel asks.

"My name is Mathúin," the man replies, and I see a flash of fangs as he straightens. My chest tightens as I look down—another vampire. "Cú Lacha sent us."

"Mathúin," Kestrel repeats softly. "What does Cú Lacha want with me?"

Mathúin shrugs, yanking open the coach door. "To meet you."

Kestrel sighs, but he enters the coach. Mathúin looks at me expectantly. I hurry in. The door shuts behind me as I sit across from Kestrel, Mathúin ordering the driver to return to the City as he climbs up next to the man. Kestrel moves to the windows immediately, but nothing is revealed behind their curtains as the coach drives directly into a bank of fog and he ends up sitting back with a frown. His frown turns into a glare the longer the coach ride takes, the more of the City that's hidden from us, and he focuses that glare on the windows. I brush dirt off my feet and pull my boots on before I try looking out the windows again, moving aside velvet and lace curtains, but still all I see is the heavy blanket of fog.

"He's hiding the City from us," Kestrel murmurs. "More power than I expected." He sighs, stretching out along his seat and throwing his arm over his eyes. "I did not plan on meeting Cú Lacha."

"What *was* your plan?" I ask. "Dazzle me with pretty sights of a City I don't know?"

"I *was* going to show you his City before we returned to yours, but we weren't going to stay here *long*. Who knows if he's like other royalty? We could be here for hours now."

He doesn't look like a god now, pouting as he sprawls across the seat with dirt and sand clinging to his legs. I smile as I watch him, but he doesn't stop sprawling until the coach comes to a halt. He sits up quickly then, mismatched eyes trained on the door. When it opens, Mathúin barely has time to step away before Kestrel is throwing himself out of the coach like he's been a bird trapped in a cage. I follow at a more leisurely pace, smiling at Mathúin's frown. The frown doesn't disappear as he gestures for us to follow him into the palace.

Like what I saw of the City before, it's a dark thing, made of cold gray stone with no banners decorating it. That sickly green light illuminates the courtyard, but there's a warmer light when we enter, old tapestries and paintings along the walls. I don't recognize the figures in any of them—there are humans and elves, even some fay, but there are just as many creatures I've never seen before lining our walk through the palace. Kestrel ignores our surroundings, padding down the hallways barefoot and silent, boots knocking against his leg. I don't let my curiosity keep them from getting too far ahead, and eventually we find ourselves in a private sitting room where Mathúin promptly abandons us.

Kestrel drops his boots noisily. "*Well,*" he says loudly when that doesn't do anything. "We're here." His voice carries around the room easily, but still no one steps from the shadows or through a door. He narrows his eyes.

"Maybe we're supposed to wait for a summons," I suggest as I drop onto a damask couch.

"Perhaps," he agrees, but he glares at everything in the room. "But if he's like others I know, he's watching us."

"Would I have had to meet him eventually?" I ask. "This Cú Lacha."

"Yes. This City is for the dead and creatures of the night. Psychopomps fall under that."

I tap my finger against the couch. "I'm not going to do what *he* says. I'm still debating on how many of *your* orders I want to follow."

"You don't have to do what he says," Kestrel replies, crossing the room to stand in front of me.

I lean towards him, smiling a little. "But I have to do what you say?"

"Ideally."

"Do all gods of death kiss their psychopomps?"

He smiles, taking my face in his hands. "Not all of them," he says. "But my gods kissed me, and I like kissing others. Do you not like kisses?"

"Oh, I adore kisses," I reply. He leans down and kisses me gently. "Your gods?" I ask quietly.

"I was not always a god," he answers, just as quietly. "And that is a story for another time."

"What is now for, then?"

He kisses me again, then sits on the couch with his legs thrown across my lap. "Learning how to be a god. Teaching you to guide souls to the realms of the dead."

"That's all?"

He shrugs. "You don't bring Death. You come for them after. You ease them into their new realm, answer questions they have."

I nod. "And Death comes with you?"

He frowns, but Mathúin returns before he can reply. The vampire stops just inside the door and points at Kestrel. "You," he says. "Cú Lacha only wants you."

Kestrel doesn't move. "And Joss?"

Mathúin glances at me. "He'll be taken care of."

Kestrel still doesn't move. "Will you take him back? To his City?"

I frown. Mathúin's head cocks to the side as he thinks, and he ends up shrugging. "It's possible. I'll ask."

"Good," Kestrel says, shooting to his feet. He kisses my cheek, hovering close as he whispers. "I'll come to you later."

I grab his wrist before he can pull away. "I shouldn't stay? You wanted me to be your companion."

His smile is so bright, so delighted. "I do, but you should go. Learn how to move between the realms first. Visit those you loved."

I let him go, not bothering to hide my doubt. Kestrel only smiles again and gestures for Mathúin to lead the way. Mathúin glances at his dirty, bare feet, but he only sighs and I watch them go silently. Once they're gone, the door shut behind them, I lean forward and put my head in my hands, between my legs, and stare at the floor. A *psychopomp*. I had no idea what I was doing with my life on a regular basis before I died, and now I'm supposed to guide the dead?

I sigh and sit up, pushing my hair away from my face. A later problem. The first problem is getting back to my City so I can talk to Dorian and Armel.

SIX

D ORIAN'S NEW HOME IS in a quiet part of
the City, ivy crawling up the brickwork
of a thin townhouse with two stories. Torches
line the street, and candles glimmering in the
windows show Dorian to be present. I stare at the
townhouse, rooted to a spot across the street.

Mathúin warned me that time had passed since
my death, but he couldn't tell me how long—time
isn't kept the same way in the City of the Dead as
it is in the City of the Living, and the dead have
no need for time. His warning has me moving
stiffly as I cross the street and hesitating before the
door to Dorian's townhouse, distractedly lifting
my hand to knock.

I place my palm against the wood instead. I lean forward, resting my head against the door. All our years with the fay, and nothing could prepare me for this. I hadn't thought of what this moment would be like while with Kestrel, and there had been no time for Kestrel to prepare me for it. *Visit those you loved.* Perhaps it would have been wiser to see Armel first, but here I am instead. I lift my head with a sigh and push my hand lightly against the door—walking between the realms is a bit of magic many nonhuman creatures can do, though neither Maiwenn nor Malo could do it. Armel merely waves his hand. How does a psychopomp do it?

I stare at the door and continue to push until my hand starts to pass through it, then don't quite breathe as my arm move through it. A sudden spike of fear has me taking a deep breath and squeezing my eyes shut as I walk through it entirely. On the other side, I grin giddily and turn around to look at the inside of the door.

A dagger lands in the wood not far from my head.

I stare at it with wide eyes, then grimace as I turn back around. Dorian holds another dagger at the ready, a thick book hugged to his chest. He looks—alarmed, grief-stricken, *angry*. "It's me," I say, throwing my hands up. "Promise."

"My brother *died*."

"Maiwenn taught us that death isn't always the end."

"That doesn't mean you're Joss."

I drop my hands as my exasperation rises. "How am I supposed to prove it? I could recite our life stories and you probably wouldn't believe me because you can be a stubborn, contrary shit. I could tell you all the things Malo whispered to me at night before things ended between us, but you *hate* hearing that. I *could* tell you you're holding that dagger wrong. Malo and Maiwenn would both be annoyed with you. They taught you better."

He frowns, glancing at the dagger. "I'm not—*whatever*." He rolls his eyes as he lowers the dagger, gripping the book tighter.

I step forward, curious about the book, and he lifts the dagger again. I pause, then roll my eyes back at him as I cross the room and take the book. It's old, worn brown leather with gold lettering framed by flora—*The Flowers and the Knight.* I smile as I run my fingers over the cover. An old book from our childhood, one we'd both obsessed over. Despite the wary look he still wears, Dorian steps closer as I open it to look at the first pages.

"Is it really you?" he asks softly.

"It is."

He drops the dagger and it skitters across the floor as he hugs me tightly, pressing the book against my chest. I hug him back as best I can. "What are you, then?" he asks into my shoulder. "Not a ghost if I can touch you. Revenant?"

Could I ever be that furious? "Psychopomp."

His head shoots up so fast he almost knocks it into mine. "A *what?* Seriously?"

I place my hand against his forehead and gently push him back. "Yes. I don't know why *me,* but a god picked me." I hesitate before I continue, glancing at him out of the corner of my eye. "How long has it been? Since I died?"

Dorian steps away, picking up the dagger and twirling it around to avoid looking at me. "Six months."

I wobble my way into a chair, setting the book aside and putting my head in my hands as I groan. "Six *months*."

"Malo hasn't been seen since your funeral," he says, so soft I almost miss it.

"Am I supposed to *care*?" I ask, lifting my head.

He stands in front of a table covered with books now, shrugging at my question. "He still loved you."

"Then why did he side with Maiwenn?" I demand.

There's a small smile tugging at his mouth when he glances over his shoulder. "Did you come back from the dead just to argue?"

I smile back. "Only with you."

He sighs, abandoning his dagger and crossing the room to sit on the floor by my feet. I run my hand through his hair as he rests his head against my knee.

"I missed you," he says. "I don't ever want to see Armel carrying your dead body again."

"I'm sorry," I murmur, leaning down to hug him tightly. "I'll try not to do it again."

He nods, squeezing my arms. "You're a terrible older brother."

"Thanks," I reply dryly as I sit up.

He twists to look at me, pulling his legs up to rest his arms on his knees. "You should make it up to me."

The way he sits, the way he looks at me so eagerly and with a small smile—it immediately makes me suspicious. "How?" I ask carefully. "What do you want?"

He grins, revealing those fangs of his. "Help me kill someone."

"Oh," I say faintly. "Is that all?" Then I frown as I consider the request. "Who? Everyone loves you. It's me they struggle with."

"Not everyone struggles with you," he replies. "Malo didn't. Armel doesn't." He gets a coy look. "That mare—Nikolay?—doesn't."

I kick his foot. "Who do you want to kill, Dorian?"

He's silent for a moment, staring at me, then says, "Mikael and the vampire that turned me."

I sit back. "Do you know the vampire's name?"

"Ask your god. Shouldn't they know? Psychopomps belong to gods of death, and you have to die to become a vampire."

"He might be too new to know that," I mumble.

He frowns. "*What?* Your god might be *too new?*"

I nod, staring at the floor. "He didn't even have a name to give me when I woke up. I bet Mikael knows the vampire's name, though. He said the vampire paid him."

"Your—" I look up. Dorian shakes his head. "Never mind. We'll come back to your god. You think Mikael actually knows the vampire's name?"

"I'd bet he contacted the vampire himself. What's Mikael been doing for the past six months?"

Dorian's smile is a cold one. "He hasn't been seen outside the family estate since we were rescued. Seems that mare broke him a bit. Might still be tormenting him, actually. I heard he's woken up screaming every night since."

I'm going to kiss Nikolay the next time I see him. "We'll have to pay him a visit at home, then."

Dorian grins and jumps to his feet. His enthusiasm is reminiscent of our years under Maiwenn's care, and my smile fades as I watch him wander through the townhouse. He enters one room, comes out attaching a sword to his belt and adjusting how it sits on his hip, then runs upstairs to noisily rummage through the rooms there. When he comes back down, he holds up a hand for me to wait before entering another room on this floor. I flip through the book as he continues his search, but set it aside when he comes out carrying a sheathed sword that I don't recognize. I recognize the belt and scabbard—years old gifts that Malo made for me himself—but the sword is not the sword I left behind. I handle it carefully, stepping closer to a candelabra to examine it. The blade is a blueish black, flecks of something in the metal reflecting the candlelight like stars, and the pommel has a single sapphire in it, the grip wrapped in dark leather. The balance is perfect when I hold it up, and I glance at Dorian.

"Elouan," he explains.

I look at the sword again before sheathing it. "This isn't like his usual work."

Dorian shrugs. "He sent it via messenger with your name on it and never answered my questions." I frown, but he's steering me to the door before I can speak. "We should get to the Trahan estate before it's too late."

"*Tonight? How* are we getting there?"

"Tonight," he says. "And you're a psychopomp. Magic us there."

"Magic us there," I echo doubtfully.

"I don't know what psychopomps can do! What have *you* been doing for six months?"

I roll my eyes. "I don't know either! I've been a psychopomp for *maybe* twelve hours! Whatever I was supposed to be taught has to wait."

That confuses him, but not for long. "Figure it out," he demands. "A coach will be too obvious."

I glare at him. "And if I've never been to the Trahan estate? What if I need that knowledge to get us there?"

He opens his mouth, then shuts it as he glares at nothing in particular and shoves past me to yank the door open.

"I have, by the way," I say. He stops and turns a baleful look on me. I smile back. "Mikael made me trek out to the estate when we were discussing the terms of my loan." He slams the door shut, crossing his arms. "Doesn't mean I know how to get us there with some psychopomp ability."

He throws his hands up as he spins back to the door. "Useless! When did you get so useless?" He pauses before he opens the door, though, looking back at me again with a frown. "How did you get in *here?* You didn't open the door."

"I went through it."

Dorian looks at the door and then me. I stare back at him, then focus on the door. Could it be so easy? Just focus as I did before? I step up to the door, running my hands over it as I remember the estate.

A beautiful villa surrounded by evergreen trees with a roof of red clay tiles, a courtyard containing a fountain statue of a man playing a lyre and cherubic angels surrounding him. Mikael had someone meet me in the courtyard and lead me to his study, where he waited for me behind a large desk. He had bookshelves all along his walls, but every book had such a coating of dust that it was easy to tell he only liked how they looked. I'd been distracted during our meeting, staring at a book on a shelf behind him—a first edition of *Saint Bleiz and the Hunt*, a book Maiwenn had gifted me a later edition of. I wanted that first edition.

I want it still.

The edges of the door glow faintly, a soft purple light that expands to cover the entire door. I step back as the door disappears entirely, the light shimmering before an image of Mikael's study appears in it. I grab Dorian's wrist and pull him through before I can think better of this.

It's *cold*, like when Armel and Nikolay rescued us from Mikael's torture, but we stand in the study a moment later. I let go of Dorian and walk around the desk immediately, grabbing the book off the shelf. Dust still coats it and I blow most of it away, then rub at the cover—green and silver, ivy surrounding two figures. One figure holds the other in a pose that reads romantic or tragic without knowing the story, both when one knows it. I grin and hold up the book to show Dorian.

He rolls his eyes. "Of course a book is what gets you to figure it out."

I lower the book with a frown. "You have your fancies and I have mine."

"Are you going to carry that around the entire time we're looking for Mikael?"

"Maybe." I walk around the desk as I flip through the book lazily. "I want to find Petran, too," I say as I stop in front of the doorway I created. I wave a hand at it, mimicking Armel, and smile as the doorway disappears.

"Why?" Dorian asks quietly as he opens the study door to peer into the hallway.

"He's the one who killed me."

Strange, how still vampires can become. Corpse still. It's unnerving to see Dorian become that still, even as he looks over at me. I don't like the reminder of what he's become, guilt shooting through me as I clutch my book tighter.

"Then we go after him as well," he says, slipping through the door.

I place my hand on my sword as I follow, keeping my footsteps light. Almost immediately, a whispering reaches my ears, faint but melodic. I pull my sword from my sheath and Dorian follows suit, but when he tries to speak I shush him as I strain to listen to the whispering. There are no discernible words, just voices on top of each other—it's almost soothing, it *could* be soothing, but there's a furious edge to the whispering that's only sharpened by the villa's silence. I wrinkle my nose up. Is this something else Kestrel should have taught me about?

"Can you hear anything?" I ask Dorian quietly. He shakes his head with a frown. I stifle a sigh and try to follow the whispers.

Something to learn about from Kestrel, then.

The whispers lead us to a room, a soft light shining under the door. I wait for a shadow to cross the light but none comes, and I open the door slowly. The room is lit by candles as if the occupant is scared of the dark—but not all of the shadows have been chased away, two corners of the room still holding shadows deep enough to hide Nikolay. I glance at them, wondering if he sits in them now, but he doesn't come out if he does. The door shuts quietly behind me as Dorian enters the room, and the lone figure in the bed whimpers quietly in his sleep. I lift my book above my head and drop it.

It lands with a loud thump.

Mikael shoots up into a sitting position, eyes wide and fearful.

"Hello," I say.

He screams.

It's cut off by Dorian appearing at his side, hand squeezing his throat. "Hush now," Dorian says softly. Mikael trembles so terribly I'm surprised the bed doesn't shake with him.

I set the book on a desk against a wall, picking up the dagger already laying there to examine it—a match to the one that killed me, pretty and deadly, with a freshly sharpened blade. Mikael watches me, breathing shallowly with Dorian's hand still around his throat. I sheathe my sword and climb onto the bed, crawling towards him. He whimpers, pulling his legs away. I smile as I shove his legs down and straddle his lap. Dorian pulls his hand away as I lean close and place the dagger against Mikael's cheek.

"How quiet can you be?" I ask. The tip of the dagger is just below his eye and he stares down at it while holding as still as he can. "I know *we* screamed, but you had us on your own estate. And in a room completely away from everyone, I assume. Especially away from the children. Are they here?"

His gaze snaps back to me. "Don't hurt them," he croaks out. Dorian scoffs as he wanders the room. Mikael glances at him, then stares at me when I press the dagger down. "Please."

"I have no interest in hurting them," I say. He sags, the blade sharp enough to cut into his cheek. I smile again as he flinches, and place my other hand at the back of his neck to keep his head close as I drag the dagger along his skin. "I have loathed you from the first moment we met. Tonight is going to be the best night of my life."

Mikael shudders, then bites back a cry of pain as I drag the blade along his entire collarbone. Blood wells up quickly, flowing across his chest and staining his nightshirt. It's a bright crimson against the white nightshirt, his pale skin; it's all I can smell, memories of my own torture rearing their head. I tear the nightshirt apart, and Mikael's breath hitches as I press the blade against his nipple. I drag it down, only slicing into him below his nipple and creating a cut that stops just before his navel. He still trembles, but he's very good at staying silent—even when I take his hand and pull his fingers back one by one until they break, the cracks and pops as loud in this room as they were in the room he held us in.

I don't know what Dorian planned for killing Mikael and the vampire—I certainly didn't have a plan when I agreed to help—but he doesn't stop me as I remember the way Cyril carved into us, how he broke our bones and ripped us apart. The whispers I've been hearing hush as I work through my memories almost methodically, only Mikael's quiet whimpers reaching my ears. He grows a little louder when I take his hand and carve it apart to reveal the inner workings as Cyril did my arm, but still no screams. His blood spreads across the bed like mine spread across the floor, but there's no Cyril here to heal him.

There's so much blood.

There was so much more blood under me and Dorian.

Eventually, I shift the way I sit and Mikael's breath catches—not from pain.

I pause.

I look down.

His cock is hard under me despite the blood loss.

I look into his eyes as I slip my hand under the blanket that covers him, wrapping my fingers around the length of him and stroking slowly. His blood makes it easy. I press the dagger against his throat as

I whisper in his ear. "Is that why you'd leave us?" I ask, squeezing. The breath he lets out is a harsh one. "Watching Cyril *work* made you want to fuck someone? Did you find your wife when you left us?" He shakes his head. I smile, resting my cheek against his. "Did you fuck him, then? Maybe he fucked you and carved into you like I'm doing. Did he heal you after?" I rub my thumb over the head of his cock until he gasps. "Answer me. Maybe I'll let you go."

"N-no, I didn't," he says, so shakily. I can't tell if it's fear or arousal that holds him in its grip.

"Didn't what?"

"I didn't—didn't—" I slide the dagger along the underside of his jaw, squeezing his cock as I do. "I didn't fuck anyone," he gasps out.

"Did you want to?"

He shakes his head, wincing as he cuts himself on the dagger.

"Tell me the truth, Mikael," I croon.

He wheezes, but then, very quietly, "Yes."

I laugh as I sit back. His eyes are tightly shut, lips pressed together. I tap the dagger against his mouth. "Open your mouth." He does so slowly, but far enough I can stick the dagger in. His eyes open immediately, wide with fear again as I rest the blade against his tongue. "You always liked coming to the club on the nights I was scheduled for the stage," I say, sliding the dagger along his tongue slowly. He swallows some of the blood that fills his mouth, the rest dripping down his chin. The dagger cuts the corner of his mouth as I pull it free. "It's very tempting to leave you with the memory of tonight."

He swallows more blood, tries to speak.

I slide the dagger into his throat.

He gurgles and paws at my arms, but his fingers are broken, skin and muscle peeled back on one hand. His strength is gone, and smeared blood makes it harder to hold onto me. I stay seated on him until the life leaves his eyes. A faint glow hovers in the corner of the room, the same whispering from before returning. When I look, there's a spectral version of Mikael standing there, hale and hearty once more. I shake my head and climb off the bed, using a shirt thrown over a chair to wipe my hands off as

I approach the ghost. Mikael only stares at me, the not-quite-there stare of someone who's struggling with perceiving the world again.

"You'll be forgotten in the realms of the dead," I tell him quietly as I pick up the book from the desk and set the dagger down again. I leave the dead behind and shut the door quietly behind me. Dorian leans against the opposite wall, arms crossed and eyes closed. "When did you leave?" I ask him.

"As soon as I realized he was getting aroused," he answers, opening his eyes.

I tilt my head to the side in the question.

"Smelled it," he says, tapping his nose.

"Oh. That's . . ."

"Annoying."

I smile a little. "Let's find his brother."

"Slow or quick for Petran?" he asks, pushing away from the wall. I shrug as I walk away, but he pulls me to a stop, looking so concerned now. "Are you all right?"

I dredge up another smile. "I'm fine."

"Joss."

"I'm fine. Let's go before we're discovered."

He sighs and gestures for me to follow him. He definitely had plans before I returned, as he doesn't stop and question himself, just leads me through the villa to another door not far from Mikael's. We pause, glancing at each other. Dorian frowns and opens his mouth.

The door swings open before he can speak, Petran swinging a sword as he runs out half-dressed.

It's only the years of training from Malo that has me able to drop the book and pull my sword up in time to block Petran's attack. He snarls as he throws himself forward, using his weight to force me back. I toss my scabbard aside as I hold up my sword, falling into a stance that Malo had been adamant about me perfecting. Strange, to think of him now, but the last time I fought anyone in earnest was him. He'd challenged my right to leave the fay, a long duel that ended with me on my knees before him. I can't—*won't*—let a fight with Petran end the same way, and I step forward as I swing my sword—

But Dorian is faster than either of us, a vampire who had six months to adjust while Petran cared for an injured man and I was dead.

The speed at which he dips down and cuts the backs of Petran's ankles almost makes me dizzy. It makes me *cold,* another reminder of what I did to him.

Petran cries out in pain as he crumbles to the ground, but I barely hear it as I stare at my brother. "*Shut up,*" Dorian hisses as he pulls Petran into a kneeling position. He stands behind Petran, draping his arms over the man's shoulders. "You know, I spent months thinking Mikael had ordered Joss's death, but then Joss told me it was *you.*"

The blood leaves Petran's face as he actually, truly looks at me.

"Hello," I say softly.

He doesn't scream as his brother did, face twisting into a scowl instead. "How?" he asks.

"I am but a psychopomp with a duty to fulfill," I say, shrugging. I lean down to put us at eye level. "But there are souls I will never guide. I will not *touch you* unless to make sure you are forgotten. You and Mikael will rot in the realms of the dead, maybe fed to those creatures that feed on the things that make our souls what they are."

He scoffs.

I place my sword against the side of his neck, against the vein there, and drag it down slowly, blood spurting out and covering my arm. Petran throws his hands up to cover the wound, meeting my gaze with wide-eyed terror.

Dorian covers Petran's mouth as he leans down to place his mouth at Petran's ear. "A vampire's bite isn't always pleasurable," he says quietly. "That was my favorite lesson. Would you like to know how it feels?"

Petran shakes his head.

Dorian bites him anyway.

He screams then, loud enough despite Dorian's hand covering his mouth that I step back.

The whispers reach for me, sticking in my mind like little burrs. I shudder and look away as Dorian feeds on Petran, rubbing the back of my neck.

Psychopomps guide the dead. We don't cause death. I'm ignoring my duties.

What will Kestrel say of me now?

Will he still want me as a companion?

I look at the blood covering my hands, then close my eyes as the whispers increase.

Someone touches my arm.

I flinch and bring my sword up.

Dorian looks at me with wide eyes. "Joss?" he asks, and it sounds like it's not the first time he's said it.

"I'm fine," I say, glancing behind him. Petran's body is sprawled across the floor now, a pool of blood under us. I pick up my book before it can get even more ruined, hugging it to my chest as I look back at Dorian. Petran's ghost stands just behind him, not nearly as lost looking as Mikael was. A furious ghost, the kind revenants are born of.

Guide the dead, Kestrel said.

I turn away from Petran to look at my brother again. A revenant would be a problem, but I doubt Petran could even summon up the energy to be dangerous as a revenant if he becomes one. Too much of parasite to create it on his own. "We should go," I whisper. Dorian nods, hand still on my arm. I start walking without thinking about where I'm going, unable to summon the energy for another doorway. Dorian silently steers me to the courtyard, gently taking my sword from me.

A short redhead in a dark purple chiton and jade jewelry falls into step with us. "I did this once," Kestrel says quietly as we leave the courtyard.

"What?" I ask.

"Revenge. I did not take kindly to people hurting those I cared about."

"Who are you?" Dorian asks.

Kestrel looks at Dorian so blankly that I can't help but smile. "Kestrel," I say. "You picked Kestrel."

"Right," he chirps.

Dorian looks at him doubtfully, then me. "My god," I tell him. He doesn't look convinced at all. I look at Kestrel again. "I take it that means you aren't . . ." I don't even know what to say. Angry? Disappointed?

Kestrel shakes his head. I take a deep breath, letting it out slowly. He takes my hand, head against my shoulder as we walk into the trees surrounding the villa. There's a road somewhere, but Kestrel leads us to a small creek instead, the noises of the night surrounding us in a peaceful juxtaposition against the blood covering me and the deaths we've left behind. I sit down next to the creek heavily, dropping my book next to me before I pull my legs up and rest my head on my knees. Two sets of footsteps approach, but only one person kneels next to me.

"Are you all right?" Kestrel asks softly, tucking my hair behind my ear.

I shake my head.

The sob isn't a surprise—it's been building, this thing hovering on the edges of my existence until now, until this peace by the creek. Kestrel pulling me into his arms *is* a surprise. It loosens—dislodges—something in me. He hums quietly, stroking my hair as I cling to him and cry. He doesn't say anything, doesn't try to tell me everything's all right, doesn't try to tell me things will be better.

Death is here, but all he does is hold me and offer a silent comfort.

SEVEN

DORIAN CLEANS OUR SWORDS silently as Kestrel holds me. My crying subsides but I don't pull away from the god, instead listening to the sounds of the forest around us as he and Dorian talk quietly about the City. Kestrel is *full* of questions—it's like hearing Dorian when he was younger and had yet to grasp the rules of living with the fay, and then again when Dorian first came to the City and had to ask me about everything all over again because he'd grown so used to the rules of the fay.

"Did you ever tell Maiwenn?" I ask abruptly. They're both silent immediately and I sit up slowly, wiping at my cheeks as I look over at Dorian. "About . . ." I look at his mouth.

He looks down at the creek as he nods and sighs. "When we told everyone about your death. She acted like we'd both died. Malo was too busy grieving you to care about what happened to me, but he's at least invited me into his demesne since then. She hasn't."

"I'm sorry," I say. I was Malo's favorite, he was Maiwenn's—but I walked away from Malo, and Dorian still spoke to our would-be mother often.

He glances at me. "What do you think they're going to say *now*? A vampire and a psychopomp." He shakes his head and stands to pace.

"I don't think Malo will care," I say, crawling over to the water to try and clean the blood off my hands. I shiver as the cold water hits me and scrub vigorously. "Not if he's already invited you back."

"True. He'll just be happy you're alive again."

I nod, glancing at Kestrel. There's blood on him from me, but he ignores it as he watches me. "What now?" I ask him softly.

"Lessons, perhaps," he replies. He stretches and now I see how his chiton reveals his legs, his arms—the parts of him covered in the marks that almost look like tattoos. Thorns, vines, and poppies along his left leg. A poppy withers as I look. Spiderwebs, raven feathers, and constellations along his arms. The constellations weaving with cypress branches across his collarbones, the bird skull at the hollow of his throat. Rose petals peek over his shoulders. Stars winking in and out of existence.

He notices me looking and gives me a wry smile.

I stare down at the creek, pulling my hands from it and waving the water away. Kestrel scoots closer to take my hands, rubbing them to help bring the warmth back. "What have you figured out tonight?" he asks softly.

"I walked through a door," I say. "I created a doorway from Dorian's home to bring us here, but I don't know how to do that again."

"Walking between the realms," he replies, nodding. "Everything you can do is based on what you *want.* You wanted something when you made that doorway. What did you want?"

"A *book,*" Dorian says, almost incredulously.

"What's wrong with that?" Kestrel asks.

Dorian shakes his head and comes to stand next to us, hands on his hips. I stare up at him—there's not nearly as much blood on him as there is on me, but I can see some of it clinging to his blond hair. He stares back, then shakes his head again. "You are *covered* in blood."

I look down at myself and murmur, "Mikael bled a lot."

Kestrel digs his nail into my palm. I flinch and look up, pulling my hands away. "It is probably wise that you do not do what you did tonight again," he says. I nod. He sighs, tucking my hair behind my ears and holding my face. "Your duty is to both Cities, do you understand that?" I nod again. "Good. You're also my connection to these realms. I need you, and that means you need to *stay out of trouble.*" Dorian snickers. I smile a little as Kestrel squishes my cheeks. "I think you need some rest," he says softly, thumb stroking my cheek. "There's a lot to teach you, but lessons can wait a little longer. I'll find you again in a few days."

"What if I want to stay with you?" I ask, taking his hands before he can pull them away.

His smile is so beautiful with those dimples. "Then I'll steal you away when I come back. But not tonight, Joss." He gets up onto his knees without taking his hands from mine and kisses my brow. "Tonight, you go home and rest," he whispers. "May you dream of beautiful things."

I close my eyes, nodding and sniffling. I feel it when he disappears between the realms, his hands slipping from mine. I open my eyes slowly and stare at the spot he used to be before I sigh and lean forward, placing my hands against the ground. Whatever I can do is based on what I want. What do I want right now?

I do want rest. I want to get Dorian home and have him be safe again, then I want to go to the club and find Armel. I want to replace his memories of me dead in his arms. I want to fall asleep next to him. I want him to tease me again and get controlling about my routine when I'm scheduled for the stage. I want to get into an argument with him about my routine and overhear Ryn betting on how we reconcile our conflicting ideas, whether we fuck it out or not. I want to find Nikolay again and give myself over to him for an entire night like I was supposed to do.

Maybe I want to find Malo again.

The purple glow is almost missed in the pre-dawn light, the doorway becoming more solid as I focus on it. Dorian's sitting room slowly appears within. "I'm going to the club," I say softly, looking over my shoulder. He sighs, but picks up our swords and comes to kneel and hug me. I hug him back, smiling sadly at how he tries to hide his sniffling as he gives me my sword. "It's going to be all right. I'm not leaving again."

"Good," he says, and he doesn't look at me as he wipes at his eyes and steps through the doorway. I close the doorway before he can turn and reveal his tears.

I wait to summon a doorway to the club. I don't want to see everyone just yet, only Armel, and they'll need time to close and clean the club.

The forest slowly lightens around me, birds waking and chirping to each other in the trees. I sit with my legs pulled up to my chest, hugging them as I rest my cheek against my knee and stare at the creek. There are no whispers now. I close my eyes and listen to the birdsong instead. They'll be eating and drinking in the club, a final meal before everyone starts to leave.

I miss Armel's fucking foxes.

Dawn has come and gone when the birds quiet and I summon a doorway to the club.

It's quiet and empty, brightly lit. Clean, though a single couch still sits in the middle of the stage. Armel lays on that couch, one arm tossed over his eyes and his other hand atop his stomach. He wears dark purple from head to toe, a color I've only seen him wear in jewelry to mourn his exile. He doesn't move as I walk through the club and set my sword and book down on a table quietly, but he stirs as

I walk up the stairs to the stage. I stop at the top, waiting as he sits up. He stares at me, inhaling deeply and slowly.

"Hello," I say.

"How?" he asks.

I look at my hands, traces of blood still on them. "I was made a psychopomp."

He stands and walks across the stage, but I don't look up until he's in front of me and taking my face in his hands. "You're covered in blood."

"It's not mine."

"I know," he says, and he bends down to lift me in his arms again. There's a doorway behind him showing that pocket realm, the grove and the cottage.

I rest my head against his shoulder, letting him carry me through the grove again. Foxes nap throughout it, one close to the cottage's door waking as Armel approaches. It goes back to sleep as we enter the cottage and the door shuts softly behind us. Again, I'm carried over to a tub full of steaming water. Again, he sets me down and gently undresses me. I'm helped into the tub and I pull him close to kiss him. He undresses and pins his hair up, following me into the tub again to help me wash away the blood.

He kisses me this time—claiming my mouth first before anything can be washed away, pulling me up against his body. His hands move along me slowly, carefully, when he takes a washcloth, and he kisses my neck. Under my ears. My cheeks. Over my eyelids. The inside of my wrists. My mouth again when he lifts me out of the tub.

He doesn't say anything until he has me laid out in front of the hearth, laying next to me and running his fingers along my side, and then he says, "Don't ever die in my arms again."

"I'll do my very best not to," I reply.

His eyes flutter shut as I stroke his cheek, then open again as he slides between my legs with a kiss to my knee. He hovers over me, kissing me slowly before nipping my lip sharply. I taste blood when I run my tongue over the spot. "A psychopomp owes me a favor," he says softly, not bothering to hide his delighted grin.

"Do I still owe you?" I ask.

"You're here," he answers. "You still owe me."

I groan, dropping my head back. He moves in quick, kissing my throat. I clutch at his shoulders and wrap my legs around his hips. "I should be able to get out of this since I *died*," I say, and bite my lip to hold back—a sigh, a moan, something that gives too much away as he grinds his hips down, his cock rubbing against me. "I'm much more worried about you getting a favor from me now."

"I'm feeling more inclined to use your connection to Nikolay than your duty as a psychopomp," he offers, licking a line up my throat before biting at my pulse point.

I scoff. "Has he been coming to the club still?"

"He has. He'll probably be there tonight."

"That's good to know," I whisper, toying with his hair.

He lifts himself up with a sigh, shaking his head as he stares down at me. "You're going to chase after him tonight, aren't you?"

I smile. "Maybe." He lowers his head to kiss my shoulder, but when he starts to bite, I squirm away. "Oh, don't do that again. Everyone already knows who owns me."

"I am merely owed a favor, nothing more," he says, but he only kisses the spot instead of bruising it. I laugh quietly and he slides his hand down my body, fingers moving along my cunt slowly. "Do I really have to give you up tonight?"

"I didn't get to say goodbye to him," I point out. "You had me in your arms."

"You *died in my arms.* I am given certain privileges after that."

I open my mouth to argue but he kisses me before I can speak, teasing me with the prospect of pushing his fingers into me. I cling to him, digging my nails into his shoulders. "You have me all day, Armel."

"Oh, very well," he says, pushing two fingers into me.

I gasp, arching under him. He leaves a trail of kisses down my chest, down my stomach, to put his mouth against my clit. His hair pins fall out as I grab his head, burying my fingers in his hair as I groan and roll my hips down. He curls his fingers as his tongue moves over me slowly, then sucks. It's always a question of whether or not he'll be lazy and take his time when he's between my legs, but he doesn't now—he's almost relentless instead, chasing after my pleasure until I'm moaning with it and holding him in place as I climax on his fingers. It doesn't take long, and he doesn't give me much time to relax before he's hovering above me again and the head of his cock is rubbing against my cunt. I pull on his hips as he kisses my jaw, smiling when I feel his grin against me and his cock is pushed in.

He goes slowly. I tug on him impatiently. He kisses me and I drag my nails down his back, making him hiss in pain. I grin and kiss him again, then push on his chest until I've got him on his back and I can move on top of him. He places his hands on my hips, guiding me down onto his cock. I don't move beyond that, staring down at him.

Dead in his arms, but here I am again.

Tears blur my vision.

"Shit," I mutter, wiping at my eyes. "Shit, shit, shit."

Armel clicks his tongue as he sits up, wrapping one arm around my waist and wiping my tears away with his other hand. "Tell me what's wrong, Joss," he says softly. I shake my head, breathing shallowly to cut off the sob that threatens to build. "Tell me."

I try to roll my hips and bring his attention back to his cock inside me, but the arm around my waist tightens and prevents much movement. He hugs me close, holding my jaw and forcing me to look at him. "I died," I whisper as I look into his amber eyes.

"Death comes for all," he replies. "But you're here now."

"How long will those nights haunt me?" I ask, closing my eyes as he kisses my nose.

"I don't know," he says, releasing my jaw.

I nod, sniffling. "Right." I look down, running my fingers over his chest. His nipples are pierced with silver and garnets today, and I pull on them gently. He doesn't quite hold back his groan. I smile and wipe at my tears again, then kiss him. "Help me start to forget it, then."

He lays me out under him again, one hand on my hip as he slowly thrusts into me. I run my hands along his chest, reminding myself of him—his strength, how it feels when he holds me because I'm alive and not because I'm dying. The way he shudders and groans again when I twist one of his nipples. He kisses me and pins my hands above my head when I try to keep playing with his nipples, using one hand to hold my wrists down. His other hand comes down along my body slowly, caressing an arm, the contours of my face. He's never balked at the two scars across my chest, and even now he traces the line of one and then the other, runs his fingers over the flat expanse of my chest as he kisses my collarbone. He kisses up my throat as his hand moves lower, across my stomach and between my legs. He nips at my lower lip again as he rubs at my clit and I arch under him when the orgasm rolls through me. I tug my hands free to bury my hands in his hair when he bites my shoulder at his own climax, his cock buried deep enough I groan.

We continue to lay together in front of the hearth after, talking quietly about all I've missed in the six months I've been dead. I ask him about everyone at the club, and he tells me the gossip about Mikael's retreat to the family estate. When I tell him I killed Mikael, that it was his blood that covered me, he grins and kisses me breathless. Then he listens solemnly to the details of Mikael's death, of Petran's. I tell him about Kestrel last, earning a laugh.

"I know who you speak of," he says, kissing the back of my hand. "I'm not surprised he picked you. You're a good fit for each other."

"How do you know him?" I ask, fighting off a yawn.

He grabs a blanket and throws it over me, bundling me up securely. "I met him when I was young, before I'd been exiled."

I shove his hands away and comfortably drape the blanket over both of us. "So, he really is a *new* god?"

"Yes and no." He bundles me up again, then sits up and tosses me over his shoulder as he stands. I grunt and try to squirm free, but I can only get my arms out and stare at his ass as he carries me around the cottage. "He's avoided this for ages. I wonder what happened to make him finally accept it."

My annoyance at being carried so keeps me silent, but he doesn't seem to mind as he carries me up a ladder to a loft. I'm tossed onto a bed, the blanket fanning out around me. Armel follows me down, scooping me up again to drop me on the pillows.

"There's an entire *bed* you could have fucked me on, and instead you fucked me on the *floor*," I say, hugging one of the pillows.

He flops onto the bed next to me with a satisfied, smug grin. "In front of the fire? Directly after a bath? You liked it." I scoff, then scoff again as he laughs and pulls me close. "Even psychopomps need to sleep," he says, kissing my shoulder. "You've had a long night, Joss."

"Tell me about the time you met Kestrel," I murmur, running my fingers over his lips.

He bites one of my fingers teasingly. "Another time."

I nod and yawn into a pillow. It doesn't take long for sleep to claim me.

When I wake much later, it's to the smell of cooking food and a fox snuffling into the pillows by my head. I shove the fox away as I sit up and it drops off the bed, then scampers down the ladder. More snuffling tells me there's another fox near the bed somewhere and I creep to the edge slowly. A blanket thrown to the floor holds the fox, who wiggles around wildly before settling. I smile at it as it stretches, then curls into a ball to sleep. Clothes wait for me on top of a chest near the bed, and I peek over the edge of the loft as I dress.

Armel stands in the kitchen, cooking as foxes dance around his feet. His hair has a fox's colors today, and he looks back at me with amber fox eyes. The only purple he wears is from his earrings. "Your sword was found in the club," he says. "I told everyone it belongs to your replacement. They're demanding to meet you before we open the doors."

I frown at him as I climb down the ladder. "Did you not replace me?"

"Never."

"I'm not that good."

He shrugs. "You're better than you think you are."

I come up behind him and grab his chest, toying with his nipple piercings to cover up my lack of a response. He slaps my hands away and pulls me in front of him. I laugh and hop onto a counter, letting him feed me as he finishes cooking. He moves between my legs then, leaning back against me as we eat. The foxes continue dancing around his feet, yipping until he throws bites of his food down to them. They all come in from outside to take over the kitchen and demand more after that—until he snaps his fingers once amidst a chorus of noises and the foxes all flee outside.

The club comes next.

I follow Armel nervously, out of the cottage and through the grove, down the stairs from his apartments above the club. In the club, I linger in shadows where no one can see me—but I need not be so nervous. They clamor for information from Armel, and he hushes them as easily as he'd hushed his foxes. He explains quietly, but we've had vampires and other strange beings working in the club before. Surprise comes, but it doesn't last for very long as they welcome me back and Armel orders them to get the club opened. He leads me into his office, pulling a second chair over to his desk and pushing me into it before he starts pulling books from the shelves.

I relax into the familiar work of managing the club, of sifting gossip from truth, Armel eventually leaving me to it so he can walk around the club. He leaves the door open, letting the noise of each performance reach me. Bawdy songs and jokes amidst dreary monologues, cheers from patrons. It takes another hour or so before my attention wanders too much and I'm leaving the office as well, walking into the main room slowly. The club is busy tonight, loud, another piece of familiarity that I can fall into. I lean against a pillar for a moment, closing my eyes as I take it all in.

Someone presses a drink against my hand and I open my eyes to Ryn's smile. I smile back as I take the glass. He kisses my cheek before he leaves me, and I sip at the dark red drink as I watch him weave through the crowd for the stage. Cranberries, orange, and pomegranate—Malo's favorite blend. I look at the bar, heart thudding in my ears, but he's not there. Only Armel, who points towards one of the balconies when he sees me looking. I turn and look along the balcony, but I don't see who he points out at first, too intent on searching for Malo.

It takes looking over the balcony twice before I see Nikolay, looking as bored as ever as he smokes and watches the stage. I don't think as I step farther into the room, and Nikolay's gaze falls on me almost immediately. The boredom leaves his expression as he stares. I look away to hide my smile, and he's watching the stairs when I ascend them. He still leans against the railing, blowing smoke into the air slowly.

There are no Chastain men near him, no sign of Yves on the balcony.

He doesn't say anything as I stand in front of him, but he does place his arms on either side of me as I lean against the railing, caging me in. I smile as I sip at my drink, and he rubs his thumb over the back of my hand. "What are you now?" he asks. "You aren't human if you're standing in front of me."

"Harder to kill," I tell him. He only stares. "A psychopomp."

"*Interesting,*" he says, moving closer to loom over me. "I haven't done business with a psychopomp. Too rare for that."

I shake my head. "I don't want a *business deal* with you."

"No?"

"You told me that you wanted me for an entire night because what you wanted to do to me would take that long," I say. "Do you still want that?" He smiles. I start to smile back before I remember what interrupted that night. "I killed Mikael," I say softly.

"I know," he replies, just as soft.

I tug on his shirt. "Were you there? In the shadows?"

He moves closer, dropping his head down to whisper in my ear. "Did you want me there?"

"Not an answer. Yes or no, Nikolay. Were you there?"

He kisses my cheek. "I was there. I was enjoying his fear before you arrived."

I set my drink aside and pull him in for a kiss, the railing digging into my back as he presses me against it. He kisses my neck after and I take his cigarette, dropping it into his drink. "No more of that if you're going to keep kissing me," I say.

"Agreed. Anything else?"

"Take me away and we can talk about it."

He steps back, summoning a doorway of shadows directly behind himself while holding a hand out to me. Those around us gasp and jump away from the doorway, but I grin. No need to think about being a psychopomp tonight, about the duties I must now learn and follow. Instead I follow Nikolay into his doorway giddily, kissing him again as I cross its threshold.

ABOUT THE AUTHOR

Jameson Hollybrook lives in the Pacific Northwest and misses living with a cat.

www.ingramcontent.com/pod-product-compliance
Lightning Source LLC
Chambersburg PA
CBHW011856300726
48970CB00009B/2816